# The 30 Years' War

Henrik Tikkanen

30-åriga kriget  *Translated by George Blecher and*

*Lone Thygesen Blecher*

*Afterword and notes by George C. Schoolfield*

*Published in 1987 by the*

*University of Nebraska Press  Lincoln & London*

This translation was
supported by grants from the
National Endowment
for the Arts and the Research
Foundation of the
City University of New York.

Originally published in
1977 by Werner Söderströms
tryckeri as *30-åriga kriget*,
copyright © by Henrik Tikkanen

Library of Congress Cataloging
in Publication Data
Tikkanen, Henrik.
The Thirty Years' War
(30-åriga kriget)
(Modern Scandinavian litera-
ture in translation)
Bibliography: p.
I. Title. II. Series: Modern
Scandinavian literature
in translation series.
PT9876.3.I37A61513    1987
839.7'374    86-8740
ISBN 0-8032-4415-0

*The Thirty Years' War*

**The goal of the military** is to create order. Without order it is impossible to wage war. An order is war's First Commandment: it is incontestable; it must be obeyed. Thus it follows that obedience is war's Prime Virtue. And although it occurs in such abundance, it can sometimes attain great heights, even creating military saints.

Such a saint was Viktor Käppärä, the soldier who never doubted or questioned orders: he was a true Finnish saint. In Finland, the soil breeds military saints the way Italy's breeds religious ones. This is because Italians are awful soldiers who depend more on God than on generals, whereas in Finland the opposite is true. It has also been said that Italian generals are inferior to Finnish ones, and that therefore the One True God tends to throw his support to the Finnish side. (God's role in war has not yet been thoroughly investigated, but it's clear that no general fails to exhort his troops to trust in Him in times of adversity. For, despite the best military order, times of adversity do occur in war.)

And Viktor did have his share of adversity during his lonely decades in the North Karelian wilderness where adversity even has a distinguished literary tradition. Runeberg has described how Paavo the peasant mixed bark in his bread, and Iki-Kianto has shown what it was like for people so poor they had to bark for their food since there was nothing to bite.[1] Adversity befell Iki-Kianto, too. His "castle in the wilderness" happened to be in the combat zone during the War of Continuation, and to save it he sent a greeting to the Russians on the back of a cigarette pack in which he informed them that the place wasn't occupied and therefore could be spared. Instead of the Russians, the Finns found the message, decided it was treasonous, and promptly burned the building down and put the author in jail.[2]

In the war that Runeberg described, Russian officers were invited to balls after they'd taken a town; Kulnev would drink champagne from ladies' slippers.[3] But this was before war became politicized; it was during its *l'art pour l'art* period. War had almost nothing but attractive sides to it, the most attractive one being when a young hero took a bullet in his chest, grew pale, and died: that wasn't just attractive; it was beautiful! Later, when war became politicized, acquiring, so to speak, a purpose, all the fun went out of it. It became a tedious duty—kill and be killed—except for the sense of honor which lingered on from bygone days, and which kept soldiers from taking to their heels.

Like the true saint he was, however, Viktor wasn't seeking honor. Oh, of course the thought had passed through his mind; every soldier thinks about medals now and then the way he thinks about a woman's private parts. But mostly he thinks about death and how he can avoid it.

Which isn't such an easy thing to do. During an attack, one runs the risk of sustaining heavy losses even though gaining great honor; and if one flees, there's always the chance of being shot by one's own officers or being executed at a later date, without honor in either case. This is why the most intelligent soldiers stay where they are, hop-

ing not to be forced to advance *or* retreat—and also hoping that the heaviest combat areas will occur somewhere far, far away. If one is lucky, that can actually happen.

It was in this hope that Viktor stayed at his post and became a national hero.

Besides, he *was* following an order. An order is an order until it's superseded by another order; nothing else can expunge it. Once a commander actually gave an order of the day in which he stipulated that any subsequent order to surrender was false even if it came from his own desk. Although he was on the losing side and the order caused much unnecessary slaughter, it was a stroke of genius that brought him honor and fame to his dying day.

The order that Viktor received was of a completely different sort; it was almost a request, delivered in a slightly guilty mumble by Master Sergeant Hurmalainen—but, because of the sergeant's position, it was clearly an order that had to be obeyed. It also became Viktor's protection against responsibility—which is, of course, an order's intrinsic intent. The order was simple. Sergeant Hurmalainen asked Viktor to stay at his post until Hurmalainen returned; he was just going back to the main troop to get himself a little liquid refreshment. He never returned.

As a sort of extra insurance to protect the battalion's north flank, Hurmalainen and Viktor had been detailed to an area where the Enemy wasn't expected to advance— yet just might for that very reason, because they'd think the area was unguarded. Several kilometers from the nearest gun emplacements, the post was so remote that the mess wagon came with provisions only once a week along a road so muddy that the wheels sometimes sank in up to their hubs. The sergeant's plan was to go back with the mess wagon so that he'd have a lift at least one way; he could walk off his hangover on the way back.

Private Käppärä wasn't afraid to be alone. As a child he'd been alone a good deal. Children who've had a strange or unhappy childhood make excellent front-line soldiers; there isn't an unhappier place than the front, all nonsense about adventure notwithstanding. As a rule it's located in a less than beautiful spot, usually in a swamp. If there happens to be anything winning about the scenery, it quickly vanishes with the help of all the various calibers of guns and artillery. It's quite depressing to watch a tree being tortured to death branch by branch.

Also, life on the front is deathly dull. Nothing happens, and yet one lives in constant fear that something might. When something does happen, it's invariably unpleasant. The need to get plastered is extremely understandable. Even Mannerheim, the commander of the Finnish armed forces during World War II, in his headquarters at Mikkeli filled his schnapps glass every day to the brim: he wasn't enjoying himself half as much as he had at the Czar's court years before as an officer of the guard.[4] The Finnish colonels and generals around him lacked manners even more than intelligence. They were just like the men in the trenches: awkward and surly, no fun at all. And the Prussian rigidity of Finland's allies, the Germans, didn't appeal to Mannerheim either. *His* tastes ran more to British superciliousness: he liked to sit beside Indian maharajahs on the backs of elephants and shoot tigers. No, everything about this war was wrong—and everything was going wrong, too. (Luckily, he didn't live to see the complete collapse of the British Empire; he would have found it as distressing as the assassination of the Czar's family.)

Now and then Mannerheim wrote out an order of the day, so lofty and with such flourishes that it was appropriate for both the present and posterity. But he himself slept on a Spartan cot that no woman could ever imagine sharing with him. Even though he was a very handsome man, no one told stories of his sexual conquests. He loved his horses and let himself be loved by the people. In addition to everything else he had ulcers, and he was always cranky and fed up with everyone.

Like Mannerheim, Hurmalainen had alcohol problems. In point of fact, they were twice as great as those of the Field Marshal. Not only did he have terrible difficulties laying off the stuff—he also had immense problems laying his hands *on* it. At the point where we pick up his and Viktor Käppärä's story, Hurmalainen had learned that the troop supply sergeant had just laid in a considerable store of booze: the mess officer told him so. The way Sergeant Hurmalainen figured it, the Enemy understood that the Finns understood that the Enemy figured that no one would be there and that therefore someone was—and so the Enemy wouldn't attack, especially since the road was in such bad shape that it was impassable. Besides, since the last retreat the front line had stabilized; now it was the Germans' turn to get theirs farther south, and Hurmalainen felt that it'd be safe to leave the position in Viktor's hands for a day or so.

He was absolutely right. The Enemy never did appear. It was the war itself that suddenly proved unreliable: it ended.

**When Sergeant Hurmalainen** climbed into the mess wagon, there was nothing to indicate that peace was imminent. The usual thudding, popping, and crashing sounds could be heard in the distance, and once in a while there was the cackle of a machine gun. Each time it cackled, teeth came flying out of its mouth, but never this far; the sergeant and driver didn't need to worry about stray bullets.

Whenever one of the cart wheels leaped over a bump or sank in the mud, the cart tilted violently, making Hurmalainen's insides slosh, putting pressure on his bladder. He got off the cart, unbuttoned his fly, and started pissing against a tree, a national custom in richly forested Finland. The wagon wheels' groaning must have drowned out the muffled report of a mortar which sounded like premature applause, and the whistle of the shell was so short that the sergeant didn't have time to take cover: only the thick spruce that he was pissing on saved him from the shrapnel exploding around him. Two more shells followed, but their whistles were drawn out like train whistles, and they detonated out in the swamp without doing any damage. Although the shells had been randomly directed at the woods, they did merit some applause: the first one hit the cart.

The sight was very depressing. Horse entrails were pouring out, and the mess private's head was missing.

9

Whatever one says, when you come right down to it heads are what human beings need more than anything else. But neither the horse nor the driver needed anything anymore, and, considering the way the horse's dead eyes were staring at the sergeant, he was glad he didn't have to look at the driver's eyes too. It's not pleasant to be with dead strangers, but it's even worse to be with people who die right in the middle of a conversation. Hurmalainen couldn't remember what they'd been talking about, what the driver's last words were. One remembers the last words of a great man, but who remembers those of a cart driver? At least Hurmalainen couldn't, even though he'd heard them only a moment before. Great men must take longer to die, thought the sergeant, who realized in the same instant how close he himself had come to dying.

Of course this wasn't the first time, but it'd occurred under other than usual circumstances. In this instance there were a few too many coincidences for it to be called a mere accident; Fate must have been speaking directly to him. But what exactly had it been trying to say?

The sergeant wasn't as superstitious as the country's President Risto Ryti (who'd run to a fortuneteller to learn Finland's future),[5] but as a soldier he believed that there was a purpose to everything that happened in war just as there was a purpose to war itself: to think otherwise was both blasphemous and unpatriotic. Thus, it was a question of figuring out what purpose these randomly fired shells had had. Had Fate wanted to spare him so he could drink with the supply sergeant, or was it trying to warn him? The question occupied him all the way to the troop. In fact, it was the first thing he brought up with the supply sergeant when they started drinking, but the supply sergeant couldn't offer an answer. Hurmalainen knew what the chaplain and his own wife would have said, but he felt their answers were, as you might say, prefabricated, and therefore unreliable.

Both Hurmalainen and the supply sergeant were married men; otherwise they'd never have advanced as far as they had. Heads of families were considered dependable, responsible: no child wanted to hear that his father had been executed as a deserter. (This was true for the working class as well, which otherwise was considered shifty, drunk, and indolent—but not cowardly; that the authorities depended on.) It was also assumed that fathers were prepared to lay down their lives so that their children could live in a free country. Just as Hurmalainen's father had laid down his life so that his child could live in a country free of oppression; he'd been shot by the Whites in a POW camp in Hennala after the Finnish Civil War.[6]

As he drank, Hurmalainen mulled all this over.

What really *is* a free country? he asked the supply sergeant.

A free country is a country where you can do whatever the hell you want, said the supply sergeant. Where you don't have to live in the same neighborhood as the rich bastards and you don't have to put your kids in schools where they learn to talk so fucking snooty that their own parents can't understand what they're saying. A free country is a country where nothing changes and everyone knows his place.

The sergeant wasn't sure that he wanted to die for that definition of freedom. On the other hand, freedom like that made one drink, and the schnapps felt awfully warm inside his stomach and made his thoughts pleasantly fuzzy.

The Russians' 1939 sneak attack had united the Fin-

nish people; that was what had created the "spirit of the Winter War." Everyone was willing to sacrifice: those who had least sacrificed everything, those who had more gave much, and those who had most felt themselves constrained to give something so as not to lose everything. But where was the spirit of the Winter War now? It was a spirit that didn't quite fit the concept of a Greater Finland; that needed longer clothes. Finns had come as liberators to Petroskoi and Karhumäki and Svir,[7] but the kinsmen they'd liberated weren't pleased. They had to be taught to love freedom, which the Finns immediately set out to do. But if they hadn't been especially fond of Bolshevik oppression, they weren't overjoyed with Finnish freedom, either. It was impossible to figure out exactly what sort of freedom they *did* want, so they had to be content with what they'd got and what had been good enough for every Finnish peasant and vagrant since time immemorial. Later, when the retreat began, these ungrateful wretches stayed where they were and welcomed the Soviet troops as liberators. Hurmalainen wondered if they were satisfied now; maybe people had to be liberated twice to understand what freedom really is. Or to understand that for a portion of humanity, the largest part, there is no such thing as freedom and never will be as long as their oppression can be put to good use.

It's amazing how perceptive one gets when one drinks, thought the sergeant. You see exactly what ought to be done, and then later, when you sober up, you see that it can't be done. Just the way the capitalists call it sobering up when the workers give up and accept their misery. . . . But now things were going to hell for the upper class as well, and Hurmalainen wondered if *they* were going to sober up. But it was highly unlikely. For hadn't Dr. Goebbels[8] proclaimed that every German who fell in battle was doing it so that Germany could live on?

What did a live country with dead citizens look like, anyway?

Clearly no one had thought of that, for the phrase continued to drive the German front-line soldiers ahead—or behind, you might say, since the Germans had a habit of walking backwards.[9] No, Hitler was through—that was obvious—and maybe the Finnish upper class was too.

Except that Hitler wasn't a gentleman. He'd never been one, either: you could see that in Mannerheim's expression when he'd received birthday greetings from the Führer on Mannerheim's seventy-fifth birthday.[10] Hitler was just a clown, and clowns perished while gentlemen endured. That's the way it's been since time immemorial.

This was the last thought Sergeant Hurmalainen thought during the war. He passed out, and when he awoke, peace had broken out.

**When Baron von Born,** the Minister of the Interior, announced that the war was over, he did so in a heavy, mournful voice.[11] In a way, he was right: the peace that greeted Sergeant Hurmalainen when he woke up was a heavy one. His head was heavy, and in his brain the bombing was still going on. But one thing was clear: he had come through the ordeal alive. He didn't feel nearly as mournful as the Minister of the Interior; in spite of his hangover Hurmalainen was actually happy. As a matter of fact, he couldn't see how things could be any worse than they'd been for the past four years—for his whole life, actually. He was a bricklayer, and now there'd be plenty of bricks to lay; there'd be plenty of work. The pay hadn't been great and probably wouldn't get any better, but at least it made more sense to build cities than to bomb them to the ground.

The sergeant was a typical example of the demoralization that accompanies an extended war. One's love of war drains away, hate runs dry, one's own life becomes more precious than the Enemy's death. All that effort and work gone to waste: it can take more than ten years to create a new will to defend one's country that also includes being prepared to attack if the need arises. That's what had depressed the Minister of the Interior so much: he could hardly be expected to worry about the fate of the Karelians when he hadn't even worried about his own tenant farmers.[12]

Sergeant Hurmalainen explained to the supply sergeant that he was in double need of a taste of the hair of the dog that bit him: once for his hangover and once for the war. The supply sergeant knew exactly what his friend was talking about, and offered him a good belt. But the supply sergeant was confused: he believed in Ministers, and he tried to figure out what he'd lost or would come to lose by peace. He'd been in charge of keeping track of the company's equipment; he'd taken even the loss of a pair of underwear personally. So it followed logically that he'd definitely lost East Karelia—and most likely Field Marshal Mannerheim's confidence in the troops—and perhaps other territory . . . and, if things went badly, even the right to self-determination. His right of determination over gear and provisions was gone. In a little while his wife would determine everything at home, and his boss on the job: the era of his own sweet power had ended.

Out of sheer sadness he offered the sergeant another belt and took a little one for himself.

The telephone rang, and the company commander ordered him to pack his things and get moving: within the hour the battalion would move to the village of Sevettilä.[13] Sergeant Hurmalainen was ordered to head up the third platoon; the platoon leader had stepped on a mine and lost his legs the day before.

Käppärä's still in the woods, said the sergeant.

I'll have to send for him and the equipment, said the supply sergeant.

So you can see that the sergeant hadn't forgot about Private Käppärä. Neither had the supply sergeant; he didn't forget even a missing pair of socks. He didn't forget that he'd been promised a Greater Finland. He'd been looking forward to a great and mighty nation; it had satisfied his need for *Lebensraum* (a German term very much in vogue before the age of overpopulation).

The supply sergeant looked out the window to see whom to assign the task of fetching Käppärä, and while he did so Hurmalainen swiped the bottle, stuck it in his knapsack, and went on his way. Luckily the supply sergeant never discovered the theft, which would have completely destroyed his faith in peace. He noticed Private Eskelinen sitting on a rock on a little hill in complete view of the Enemy. What an idiot, he thought at first, but then he remembered that it was peacetime and decided to send Private Eskelinen to get Käppärä. He stepped outside and went over to the private, who was sitting and smoking a cigarette, lost in thoughts that were fated to remain unknown to posterity. For in the same instant that the supply sergeant opened his mouth to give the order, the rock on which Eskelinen sat was hit by the direct fire of an antitank gun, and both were killed instantly.

It appeared that owing to the same failure to communicate that had brought about the war itself, no one had understood exactly when the truce would go into effect, and the Finns had begun the ceasefire one day too early. Of course the pages of history can still be rewritten, and perhaps this time the Finns may accuse the Russians of having begun a day too late, but that is a small matter next to much larger ones. For now, people only point out that the Russians were as undependable as they were at Pardala when they disrupted Sandels's dinner by launching an

attack an hour too early.[14] The least one can expect of an Enemy is punctuality.

It should be obvious by now that the Finnish armed forces were in no way to blame for the fact that Private Käppärä was never recalled from his post and thus never learned that the war was over. It was simply the Almighty's inscrutable strategy in managing the affairs of His Chosen People that He left one undaunted Finn to fight against their archenemy.

This, then, is the story of Viktor Käppärä, who stayed where he was—and earned an even more brilliant place in history than the one Paavo Nurmi earned by running faster than anyone else.[15]

**Before we**—with the aid of all the available documents—study our hero's subsequent fortunes (his country's subsequent fortunes, one could even say) we must first accompany Sergeant Hurmalainen to Sevettilä, where he brought his platoon—or, more accurately, where his platoon brought him. During the march he refreshed himself frequently from the bottle he'd stolen from the supply sergeant, and when he arrived at the school where the unit was to be billeted, he was feeling no pain.

This latter circumstance wouldn't be worthy of mention had it not been that in this particular instance it was to have dire consequences for the sergeant, the repercussions of which were to affect Käppärä's fate in a manner which might justify one's saying that alcohol played an important role in the eventual outcome. Indeed, alcohol has influenced most of this thirsty little country's history; very few teetotalers have had anything to do with it.

The colonel who was the recipient of the sergeant's slurred report of the unit's arrival was far from being a teetotaler himself. Instead of being drunk, however, he was hung over, and had just received one shot of B vitamins and another of uppers and downers: his usual morning medicine. The colonel believed, you see, that his position required him to celebrate every victory and drown every reversal in spirits, and what with one or the other he hadn't had a sober moment during the whole war.

In the event that his own front was quiet, he turned to battles in more distant theaters of war. Once, in fact, he'd celebrated the taking of Singapore by the Japanese, and another time he passed out with the name El Alamein on his lips.

To the colonel the armistice was an unmitigated catastrophe, but nevertheless he couldn't tolerate a subordinate appearing drunk on duty before noon. That this subordinate was also a noncom meant that it was not only possible but likely that he had *celebrated* the coming of peace instead of grieving over his country's defeat. This was a situation any self-respecting commanding officer could not accept, and he bellowed that he could have the sergeant court-martialed. Putting mercy before justice, however, he would demote him to buck private instead.

This was quite a blow. It was obvious that the colonel didn't understand how much easier it was to become a colonel than a sergeant, and how much heavier the responsibility of a sergeant was than that of a colonel. A colonel gave an order to attack or counterattack and then calculated the probable losses in percentages. But these percentages were the sergeant's friends, his responsibilities. He had to mourn the dead and assemble the wounded after first having sent them to their destruction—which the colonel might just as well consider a triumph as a fiasco. And colonels weren't demoted, they just had nervous breakdowns; they weren't held responsible for cowardice in the face of the Enemy. Now that Hurmalainen was demoted to private he'd be thought of as cowardly; he'd be discharged with the rank of coward.

Paralyzed almost to the point of sobriety by the news, Hurmalainen listened as the colonel spoke and, slow as a rising sun, the truth of the underlying nature of things began to dawn on him. In the war in which his father had fought on the Red side, the Whites had won and his father had been executed ignominiously. In the war in which he'd fought on the White side, the Reds had won and he'd been demoted ignominiously. Whatever the workingman did, it always came out wrong: for someone like Hurmalainen there was no justice—there couldn't be—and it didn't comfort him at all when, months later, several aristocrats who'd been convicted of war crimes were forced to move their easy chairs to prison for a while where they could sit in peace and quiet and write their memoirs. Actually, their stay in prison made them martyrs, which undoubtedly could be regarded as the high point in their political careers. Mannerheim—who'd been described by the Russians as a butcher and crook—became President; defeat was the high point of his career, too. When the bricklayer realized all this, he instantly lost his faith in Stalin; he'd only gone after old Party comrades and other Communists and couldn't be bothered with the bigwigs and the capitalists. In fact, he proceeded to do the capitalists a great service by forcing Finland to build up an industry that was able to finance the war reparations; the number and power of the captains of industry increased.

To Hurmalainen, however, the rapidly rising standard of living seemed an insult to the willingness he'd shown to lay down his life to save his country from defeat: no, he refused, simply refused, to lay bricks for a rotten society that duped the gullible and fleeced the poor. Instead of laying bricks, he'd drink.

He went to the capital and joined the army of "furniture polish drinkers"[16] that soon swelled to the same size as the brigade he had served with during the war; this sad army simply continued to freeze and starve and suffer and die without a soul even noticing. They fought for sympathy and understanding, but the more prosperous the society around them became, the less they got. The first winter Hurmalainen's legs were frostbitten while he slept in a sand bin and one leg had to be amputated; this made life a little easier for him. Now he could sit by the entrance to a shopping arcade and show his stump and military passport that listed all the battles he'd served in, and no one doubted that he'd lost his leg in the war. He earned quite a lot of money for booze as long as people remained animated by patriotic spirit.

Then a group of young radicals appeared, claiming to fight for the rights of society's outcasts, and managed to get a lot of attention and get voted into Parliament; afterward, when they didn't need the furniture polish drinkers' help anymore, they lost all interest in them. Unfortunately, the people identified the army of drunks with the radicals, and their generosity immediately dried up. The drunks had to make do with methylated spirits, and when the authorities noted the increase in consumption, they raised the required level of methyl so high that anyone who drank it went blind or died.

Hurmalainen responded by draping himself with all the medals he'd received for bravery, and for a short time his income soared; now he didn't have to drink the worst of the substitutes—he could treat himself to a few bottles of eau de cologne every day. But he also stirred up a lot of bad feeling among former officers who urged him to pull himself together. They told him that the Finnish soldier could lose his arms and legs, his eyes and testicles, his wife and job, but he still had no right to conduct himself in a manner unbefitting a soldier. They got the Police Commis-

sioner on their side, and the whole police force set out to clean up the city to avoid seeing the human refuse of war. This refuse wasn't nearly as decorative as the heroic dead under their arrow-straight rows of white crosses at Hietaniemi Cemetery,[17] where they rested near their beloved Field Marshal Carl Gustaf Mannerheim, who'd never given an inch during the war but who afterwards retreated all the way to Portugal when he realized that he might be held responsible for his actions.

Hurmalainen and his friends took up residence by the cemetery wall, but if any of them went inside to use a smooth stone as a pillow under his head while sleeping off a bender, he'd be kicked out. Asleep, they all looked dead, and no one wanted to think about death in a place dedicated to commemoration and resurrection. Even a baron who had installed himself in the little mausoleum on his family plot was kicked out when he scared the wits out of an attendant by sticking his ghostly face through the latticework gate to the empty room intended solely for the family pride, not their black sheep.

Then one day a miracle occurred.

Hurmalainen had been sleeping under a tree in a square where the Salvation Army happened to be holding a meeting. He was awakened by such a fierce drumroll and trumpet blast that he thought the war had started again. He looked at the tree and relived the incident with the shell and the tree, and now his foggy brain finally realized what Fate had been trying to warn him against.

Booze.

From that moment he couldn't keep a drop down even if he drank from a Coca-Cola bottle with his eyes closed: after the first gulp it all came up again. It was as if the Holy

Spirit had decided to dedicate Itself to guarding his stomach. After a few months in a sanitarium he was ready to move home to his wife, Esther, in Vimpele.[18] He was a new man, and his wife said that the new man was better than the old one even though there *were* a few little problems with potency and reasoning ability. The important thing was that he keep sober and make good money.

Which Hurmalainen did. Nothing is as dear to a Christian's heart as a lost soul who returns to the fold. The reformed bricklayer got a good prosthesis and worked on one church building after another. Materially he did not want, but the spirit that had taken up its position at the gateway to his stomach quickly extended its bridgehead and before long filled the whole man. On most issues he became as intolerant and uncompromising as his fellow True Believers, but to their sorrow his belief in a strong military never returned; he didn't even want to hear about war again. This fact was to have serious consequences in the Viktor Käppärä affair.

**Probably we shall never know** the whole truth of Viktor Käppärä's thirty years in the wilderness. If we hadn't had access to his letters (which were never sent), we would know little about the psychological effects of his long period of isolation. Fortunately, he continued to write to his mother, perhaps in the beginning in hopes of eventually sending the letters, and later, when he'd given up hope, as a sort of diary—or even as therapy.

It was only after application had been made to the Attorney General that the army gave permission to private scholars to make use of the letters and other material in the Käppärä case. The Chiefs of Staff tried to explain that the documents could jeopardize the country's relations with foreign powers and therefore wanted to classify them. The real reason was that they wanted to be the first to come out with an official version that would serve patriotic aims and support the case for a strong military. The head of the Joint Chiefs of Staff went through the Writers' Union membership list to find a new Runeberg for the job. The results were disappointing; every poet of any conceivable level of talent proved to be more or less Leftist.

Then they arrived at the brilliant idea of using a team of authors made up of a psychiatrist, a lawyer, and a priest. They were assigned the task of assembling the most careful report possible, one that would be considered so reliable that later versions would seem like misrepresentations or unchecked fantasies. The General Staff felt sure that the team of authors would find the Truth, since all three had belonged to the Commission of Inquiry into conscientious objectors and had a great deal of experience coming up with arguments against defeatism and pacifism. Their mandate was no more specific than to "clarify" the causes of the extraordinary loyalty and unsurpassed valor which Private Käppärä had demonstrated—and which was characteristic of the Finnish soldier in general.

While the work was in progress, an effort was made to keep other parties from interfering, but when the final phase of the case aroused world attention, the insistence on secrecy became inappropriate and, despite its patriotic disposition, the Attorney General was forced to reject the army's plea for classification. Also, when Käppärä was charged with murder, it became difficult for all the secret details of the case not to be made public. Therefore, the authorities decided that the whole affair might as well become a matter of public record, and they put their trust in the fact that traditional patriotic values would prevail in the assessment of Käppärä's actions. The public hadn't liked the charges against Paavo Nurmi for violating his amateur status by accepting money, and it would surely not pay much attention to a couple of murders which, under the circumstances, could be regarded as virtually legal. Patriotism, courage, a sense of duty, willingness to sacrifice, privation, and perseverance would surely outweigh a few little blemishes, particularly since Käppärä died a war hero's death.

The allegations that he died a natural death were dismissed on the grounds that a soldier who perished in battle necessarily died a war hero's death whether he intended to or not. During World War I a French regimental commander was hit by a bullet while he was mounting a prostitute in a cornfield near Verdun and nevertheless traveled to his grave on a gun carriage like any other hero of rank. The same bullet also killed the whore without making her into a heroine; had she been part of the military, of course, it might have been a different story.

In any case, the regimental commander's death set a precedent. Those who died while a battle was in progress and who were within range of the Enemy were heroes regardless of the cause of death. And Viktor Käppärä certainly drew his last breath in the heat of battle, so there could be no doubt that a hero's life ended with a hero's death, just as it should. (Since missiles and other long-range weapons have entered the picture, an international commission has updated the regulations concerning a "hero's death" to include death within a radius of the maximum range of a five-inch howitzer calculated from a battle's estimated midpoint. That the clear majority of victims in the wars after World War II have proved to be civilians only underlines the fact that the status of a "hero's death" is due only to those in proper military uniform. The prostitute at Verdun again serves as excellent precedent in this regard.)

There were much more trivial things than a hero's death and its rewards that occupied Viktor all those years, and all of them had to do with staying alive. Occasionally there were also more serious matters: he wrote an (unsent) letter to his mother saying that in his isolation he missed not only other human beings but the humanity in himself as well.

Actually, it appears from Käppärä's correspondence that, ironically enough, he regarded Sergeant Hurmalainen as his hero and idol; this came as an unpleasant surprise to Viktor's biographers, who knew all about the ex-sergeant's subsequent actions. The fact that he later became a Believer would have compensated for most of his actions had he not persisted in being a pacifist, which wasn't proper for a true Christian. Everything would still have worked out perfectly if the sergeant hadn't been alive. The three authors could easily have doctored his career into one worthy of a hero's admiration, and his relatives would hardly have protested. The deceased can be provided by history with whatever lofty qualities it cares to ascribe; this process starts right after death, with the graveside eulogies. But Hurmalainen the bricklayer was filled with a passion for truth that brooked no exaggerations. In an interview in a weekly magazine he called himself an old boozer and fornicator who had finally seen the Light. Furthermore, he said that many times during the war he'd been so afraid that he'd shat in his pants.

That hadn't prevented Viktor from admiring him. The sergeant's equanimity had filled him with a sense of security, and his broad generosity warmed the heart of the boy from the islands. Adversity and seclusion had made people in Viktor's hometown small-minded and bitter, and when they weren't complaining they usually sat and brooded by the stove or in the cabins of their boats. But the sergeant had actually *asked* to take Viktor along with him for company. He had said to the company commander that he could teach the kid a thing or two, and though the company commander had easily seen that what the sergeant wanted was a fisherman (the outpost was on a beach by a lake), he'd seen nothing wrong in getting a chance to eat fish after years of a monotonous diet, and he'd smiled and said that they shouldn't forget their fishing tackle.

While Viktor fished, the sergeant taught him everything he knew about women; and his conquests were so numerous that Viktor honored him as a hero many times over.

He himself had come close to fucking only once, but nothing'd come of it.

About the art of waging war the sergeant said that the only thing worth learning was how to stay alive. And that therefore one had to be alert—keep one's eyes and ears open. An individual man's courage was useful to the war effort, but not to the individual himself, who thereby greatly reduced his chances of surviving. The dead did not get new opportunities to demonstrate their courage, and besides, the medals usually went to those who gave orders calling for courage and bloodshed—rarely, of course, their own.

Viktor soaked up every word and took them to heart; that he survived as long as he did he could thank the sergeant for as much as he could thank him for his sex life. The sergeant's salacious stories provided him with solace and jerking-off material in times of extreme loneliness. And yet the sergeant's cynical outlook on life no doubt had a deleterious influence on our hero. The three authors might have wished that he (Viktor) had stayed a little more innocent; it might have helped in connection with the killing of the woman at Lengunperä which the Communists characterized as murder. The attorney assured his coauthors that there wasn't a court in the nation that would convict a hero of Viktor Käppärä's stature. And should public opinion begin to lean in that direction (because of political pressures from the East), one could always say that Käppärä had fallen victim to temporary

derangement of the senses due to hunger and privation. This no one would dispute.

Viktor remembered that he'd heard three explosions right after the sergeant left, but he didn't even consider that the sergeant had been hit. After all, he was with the mess wagon, and if they didn't discover that the sergeant was missing, they'd surely miss the horse and wagon. And if the horse and driver managed to get through, the driver would tell them about Viktor, and they'd send another man as the sergeant's replacement. So, after a week or ten days, Viktor began to think that his friend had taken the war away with him. It was obvious that it had moved to another spot; he couldn't hear it anymore. The thud of exploding shells and the moronic cackle of machine guns were gone, and the forests were as quiet as a listening ear.

Since the war hadn't come his way, the Enemy must have been driven back again, and the front lines shifted to the east. Viktor realized that this phase of the war must have been so important that they needed the sergeant elsewhere; after the pressure eased, they must have felt they needed only one man at this post. Viktor wondered if he should feel flattered by their confidence in him, but when no provisions arrived he knew for sure that they'd left him there because they knew he could take care of himself. He was happy that he'd taken along good fishing tackle and plenty of ammunition. In addition to his own rifle, he had the sergeant's automatic pistol, hand grenades, and a flare gun. With these he could manage for a long time, even to the final victory that Mannerheim had promised: when Karelia was liberated, the Field Marshal would sheath his sword just as he'd promised to do. Viktor decided that *he'd* fire off a rocket.

What troubled him a little was that he'd never remembered to ask the sergeant which side of the old border they were on. But it didn't really matter—as long as the new border of Greater Finland would be far to the east, along the Urals or at least from Ladoga to the White Sea.[19]

**From Viktor's letters** one can easily see that he grew very tired of being alone—especially in the beginning before he got used to it. In those moments he would gladly have disobeyed his orders if he'd known which way to head. He didn't want to run after the advancing army and expose himself to the variety of dangers of an attack, and he couldn't go home either. If he did so, he'd be caught and shot as a deserter.

All he could do was stay at his post and wait to be relieved. It looked like he'd be waiting right until the final victory. It surprised him that his outpost was still considered important enough to be manned even though the troops had advanced far beyond it. But then he remembered that the sergeant had warned him about infiltrators, terrorists dropped by plane dressed in Finnish uniforms or civilian clothes. Obviously, the advancing army had to protect its rear.

Such thoughts recur often in the letters. The psychiatrist considered them perfectly normal; they were the result of idleness, perhaps the soldier's greatest enemy, and they made Viktor's decision to stay at his post doubly admirable. (In this regard the biographers cite Väinö Linna's heroic epic, *The Unknown Soldier,* in which it's evident that the Finnish fighting man's affinity for complaining has no negative influence on his performance in battle; quite the contrary.)[20]

They had arrived at the outpost at the end of the summer, and because it was still warm and beautiful they lived in a tent they'd put up in the shade of a huge beach alder. But as autumn advanced and it got chillier and damper, Viktor had to go looking for a better place to live. He made longer and longer sorties until he finally found an overgrown foundation of an old building farther along the beach. Then, a little way in the woods, he stumbled onto the house's potato celler, which was roomy and sound; he fixed it up into a cozy little dugout, which would be his home for the rest of his life. He built a fireplace and made simple but practical furniture. For a lookout post, he built a sort of stone parapet in front of the potato cellar's door; when he looked out over the lake, he felt as well fortified as if he were behind the Atlantic Wall.[21] Soon he was living as comfortably as he had in the fishing cottages in the outer islands, and when he found an old skiff that he managed to make seaworthy, he felt that his life was complete.

The lake was full of fish but it was as enclosed as a bucket, and Viktor sometimes longed for the vast ocean that allowed one's thoughts to wander off to exotic lands just by looking at it. At the end of the last century his mother had gone to America on the other side of the ocean. She'd stayed ten years and saved up enough money for a return ticket and a pancake skillet. But she'd also had the good fortune to get a job as a housemaid in the home of J. P. Morgan himself, who, while already quite rich, got even richer by successfully campaigning to involve the U.S. in World War I, thereby making enormous profits in armaments.

Viktor's mother got the pancake skillet at a discount because it was manufactured in Morgan's factory; it was cast-iron and as heavy as an anchor. In addition to making pancakes, it was also meant to be used as a weapon; set-

tlers' wives clobbered Indians over the head with it. In the World War they drilled a hole in the bottom of the pans and used them as shields for tank machine guns.

The Morgan pancake skillet and her elegant circle of friends—footmen in livery, butlers in morning coats—had made Viktor's mother somewhat haughty, and she regarded her marriage to Viktor's father as a mismatch. Viktor's father had never been anywhere, though during Prohibition he did have his day, too: once he'd had 50,000 liters of liquor hidden in barrels, and if he hadn't started drinking them himself, he would have been rich.[22] Viktor's mother never forgave him for that; she said she should have stayed in America and married Al Capone, who at least had sense enough to watch his drinking.

Into this disharmonious marriage Viktor had been born on February 22, 1922. To avoid hearing his parents fight, he'd go down to the beach and daydream, looking out over the vast ocean: it could be calm or angry but never inconsistent or unfair, like grownups. For him the ocean represented freedom and independence and a door to the Big World—exactly as it had for Peter the Great when he built Petersburg by the Gulf of Finland and made it the capital of Russia. Right up to World War I, the Russians had coastline from the Torne River to the Courland Lagoon,[23] but after the war there was no more water at the mouth of the Neva than could fill Lenin's pocket.

Seen in this light, the Bolsheviks' wish for a seaport wasn't unreasonable, and the longer Viktor stared out across the blue eye of the lake, the better he understood them. Viktor realized that the only solution would be to drive them back behind the Urals so that they'd completely forget the taste of salt water.

**The following** is from an undated letter (most of them are, obviously because Viktor lost track of time):

*Dear Mama,*

*I just killed two of the Enemy. They are the first people I ever killed. At first I didn't feel anything, but then for a long time I couldn't sleep. Whenever I closed my eyes I saw them. To kill someone means to live with them forever. If I'd known that I wouldn't have done it.*

Viktor Käppärä expressly uses the word "Enemy." In other sentences, to be sure, he calls them "people," but he experienced them primarily as "Enemies." This alone exempts him from all charges of murder: in war one can't murder one's Enemy; one only does one's duty. The fact that he was somewhat uneasy about it is attributable to the lack of day-to-day discipline that keeps a soldier's disposition on an even keel. That he continued to suffer from insomnia and nightmares for a long period *after* the incident was no doubt caused by his isolation, which prevented him—unlike his comrades-in-arms—from talking away his "burden of guilt." (Here the biographers use quotation marks to distinguish between legitimate killing in wartime and the Biblical injunction "Thou shalt not kill," which at times does give soldiers a guilty conscience. Of course the combatants fail to consider that by killing an Enemy soldier, they are in fact sending him to a coveted hero's death, an event pleasing to Our Lord. And it is universally known that a hero's chances of entering the gates of paradise without any formalities whatsoever are incontestable.) The familiar male boasts about blowing an Enemy to bits, tearing him to pieces with a bayonet, etc., should be regarded not as evidence of a soldier's bestial nature but as a normal and healthy way for him to let off steam after a battle; Viktor Käppärä lacked this avenue of releasing tension, which accounts for the psychological imbalance one observes in the letter.

Nevertheless, it is out of the question that he should have considered himself a murderer. He had his orders and behaved in accordance with clear directives. The incident was obviously of a military nature, and all attempts to politicize it are, in the opinion of the biographers, doomed to failure.

Those who accused Viktor of murder observed that the deceased were not in uniform, were not armed, and one of them was a woman. In addition, she happened on this occasion to be naked.

All this is true. When Viktor looked in the window, she was washing herself in a big basin on the cabin floor. But, according to the experts from the Joint Chiefs of Staff and the War Academy, after Viktor had taken over command of his post and noticed that the arena of combat had evidently moved into his (unknown) sector, he quite rightly assumed that his sphere of authority and responsibility had expanded.

To find food, Viktor had been forced to wander around quite a bit. During the winters he'd set traps for rabbits, and as time went on he'd had to rove farther and farther from his outpost in search of game. One fall day when he'd gone out on the bog to pick cloudberries he noticed some buildings in a wooded glade that he at first assumed were a deserted farm. Nevertheless, he approached the house following all the proper military precautions: at the beginning he ran in a crouch from bush to bush, and for the last stretch he crawled on his hands and knees till he reached the main house.

A spotted farm cat was sitting on the porch. It stared at him, astonished.

Centimeter by centimeter he raised his head until his nose bumped against the window sill. Then he peered into the house—it wasn't deserted! A woman was sitting in a tub in the middle of the room washing herself, and by the table sat a man in shirtsleeves eating a sandwich cut from a loaf of sourdough rye bread. He was spreading gobs of butter on the bread, and under the roof beams more loaves of bread were hanging from a pole. Viktor felt sick. He had to get down on his knees and throw up in the currant bush before he could bring himself to look in again. He wasn't sure what upset him more, the naked woman or the bread. At first he felt a wave of indignation over the unfairness of it all—the man had both the bread and the woman, and he didn't have either—but this was soon followed by a strong jolt of confusion: what the hell should he do? Were they the Enemy? What else could they be?

The man sitting at the table wasn't wearing a uniform, but he was Viktor's age and he couldn't be a civilian; moreover, infiltrators were known to dress in civilian clothes. And Viktor knew that in the Soviet Army there were female soldiers; and a woman in the Finnish army would never take a bath naked in front of a man. Also, there was something especially immoral about watching a naked woman while eating a sandwich. No, they just had to be Communists.

This was one decision Viktor had to make on his own; there was no commanding officer around from whom he could ask advice. And Viktor knew that he couldn't go on living near them; sooner or later it'd be a question of either him or them, and the next time perhaps they'd be the ones to catch him off guard.

He had to attack.

Viktor bounded up the steps. The cat jumped down and Viktor kicked the door open and pointed the rifle at the couple and shouted, Hands up!

Startled, they gaped at him.

What the hell is this, the man said. Can't you knock first?

They spoke Finnish. Infiltrators often did.

Get 'em up, Viktor shouted again.

The man at the table began to boil. He asked Viktor who the hell he thought he was and Viktor said he might ask the lady and gentleman the same thing if in fact they were a lady and gentleman, which he strongly doubted. He asked if they were married to each other. No, they weren't but as far as he was concerned, said the man, that was none of his business. And Viktor replied that *everything* in this sector of the frontier was his business; he was in charge of guarding it.

Then a smile spread over the man's lips. Take it easy, guy, he said. You don't have to stay in hiding anymore. The war's been over for five years.

You're lying, said Viktor.

No, it's really true. You can go home now. There's nothing to be afraid of.

Are you a Communist?

Both of us are, said the man. You can count on us.

Viktor fired a shot into the roof and roared once more for them to put their hands up. Frightened, they did as he said. The woman got up and stretched her hands high and Viktor looked at the tufts of hair in her armpits and between her legs and at her heavy breasts and wide hips and quivering buttocks and fat thighs, and he grew faint and had to marshal all his self-control so as not to fall to his knees before this pine-soap-smelling goddess of sourdough rye. He felt an irresistible urge to give up; only the murderous look in the man's eye made him reconsider.

Then the man asked Viktor if he'd escaped from some kind of nuthouse: any fool who'd shoot a gun off indoors obviously couldn't be smart enough to desert during the war. To that Viktor replied that he certainly had no intention of deserting, especially at the suggestion of Communists. The man yelled in exasperation that if he didn't get out *right now* he'd report Viktor for attempted rape and invasion of privacy. This kind of talk was bewildering; it wasn't at all what Viktor had expected from the Enemy. Again, he had the strongest desire to sit down on the bench and suggest that they talk things over calmly. Something just wasn't right. But the next moment he realized that these infiltrators had been trained in psychological warfare and they were doing all they could to disarm him by confusion. He steeled himself against the temptation to surrender and stick his head like a rabbit into the bush between the woman's legs.

After a glance at Viktor's emaciated body and hungry look it occurred to the man that Viktor must have escaped from a prison for the criminally insane and was out to rob them. So, with his hands already raised, he grabbed half a dozen loaves of bread and threw them at Viktor, shouting that he could take their bread—that was all they had.

Viktor got it all wrong. As the bread came flying at him,

he fired a shot that went through the man's chest, sending him sprawling across the table. The woman started screaming, and in the heat of the moment Viktor couldn't think of any other way to shut her up than to give her a blast, too. With a splash she crashed back into the tub, where the water turned red from the streams of blood pouring out of her body.

The man wasn't quite dead yet. He looked at his dead woman and mumbled something about living in a world where poor people had to kill one another, and after he said that he was completely dead and everything seemed so incredible it felt as though it had never happened. Only after Viktor ate a sandwich did he know for sure that it was really true; with the taste of rye bread in his mouth he understood what he'd done and thought of the Lord who gave him his Daily Bread. He didn't think this was the best way of doing it, but in wartime maybe God exchanged the Sweat of One's Brow for the Blood of One's Neighbor. Viktor wondered if the Enemy qualified as one's Neighbor; in any case, these were his first Neighbors, and he hoped there wouldn't be any more . . . but, as so often happens in war, it was a vain hope.

Viktor wondered why the infiltrator hadn't lied more consistently. He'd said that the war was over and that wasn't true. But he'd also said that he was a Communist and that was obviously true. The very fact that he was a Communist proved that the war couldn't be over, for it was unthinkable that there'd be a Communist in Finland *after* the war. So although Viktor had been fully justified in destroying the Enemy unit, he'd still blundered; he should have interrogated them before executing them. (The word "execution" didn't appear in the official ac-

count of the Käppärä case. There they merely talked about the "Enemies who fell at Tuokojärvi.")[24] Then perhaps he might have learned how far the Finnish troops had advanced. But they probably would have lied or passed on the lies their propaganda agencies had given them.

In any case, the fact that the Enemy had turned up in this sector meant that he was still needed; obviously, the area was strategically crucial. At the same time that this realization frightened Viktor (one day more infiltrators might turn up!), his otherwise lonely war also felt less frustrating. He looked at the woman who'd just reminded him of a fruit-laden apple tree that he wanted to climb, and with horror he shuddered at the changes that death brought about so quickly. The naked corpse in the water was so sexless now that he felt his prick shrivel up in his pants; and at the same moment he felt an irresistible urge to ask his mother's forgiveness for something.

He burst into tears.

Then, completely beside himself, he poured the household alcohol over the floor and set fire to the shack, which burst eagerly into flames. Only when the room was a sizzling sea of fire did it occur to him that he was burning up food and things he badly needed, and he began to grab anything within reach. He managed to get a pair of round loaves of bread and a tub of butter and some completely useless objects that lay at the end of the table next to where he was standing. He rolled the stuff in a newspaper that the dead man had been reading while eating his sandwich. The fire had already engulfed the woman and lit her hair, and the flames breathed life into the white teeth that were bared in a death-grin, making her look as if she were silently jeering at her assassin. Viktor threw himself out-

side, his body chilled with sweat in spite of the heat from the fire.

Though it was absolutely clear that he did what he did in complete terror, later he justified the arson (naturally, it wasn't called that in the report) to himself by reasoning that it was necessary to destroy the Enemy base and its resources (which was exactly how the military expert interpreted this phase of the operation). Personally, he hoped that because of the destruction, potential reinforcements would turn back, or at least choose another, safer place (for all parties).

He was still quite shaken when he got back to his potato cellar and with trembling hands made a fire in the fireplace. His hands shook so much that the match went out, and so as not to waste too many others, he lit the newspaper that he'd used as wrapping and put it next to the firewood.

His glance happened to fall on a quickly charring headline concerning the heavy fighting in Korea; the Communists were being driven back. Completely paralyzed, he stared into the flames that had, in spite of everything, enlightened him greatly. So the war had moved all the way to Korea! It would take *ages* for the boys to march home after the war was over! On the other hand, if they were about to drive the Communists into the Pacific, the end was near.

So he ended up feeling hopeful. As so often happens in war, it was a vain hope.

**There were several mentions** of the deceased in Tuoko-järvi in the records of the county sheriff. He had written about them to the district police chief and had also kept a sort of diary of all the suspicious elements in his district. From the very beginning he'd found those two particularly suspicious.

They were city people who'd moved to the country. Why?

The man had put in for a land grant and had got it in a border district. Why?

They lived together without being married. Why?

They were Communists and didn't try to hide it.

There was an answer to all three questions. They were spies and that's why they were living near the border and they lived in sin because they were immoral (like all Communists) and they didn't keep their ideology secret so that they'd provoke the local populace (which was 100 percent patriotic) into doing something that would give the Russians an excuse to come to the aid of their comrades. The sheriff had figured this out all by himself and he'd passed on these suspicions to higher authorities. But, true to the Peter Principle of high-level incompetence, the government had ignored his warnings, and now this had happened: the house they'd lived in had burned to the ground, and in the ashes they'd found two corpses, which were undoubtedly those of the Communist couple.

It was the fire that had caused the crime to be discovered. If the fire department hadn't gone to put it out, no one would have bothered to go anywhere near the traitors (though the sheriff was the only one to use this word, the biographers implied it, too); and when the firemen found the charred bodies, they called him in. He'd conducted an investigation and called in the district medical examiner to do a post-mortem on the bodies. The district medical examiner confirmed the sheriff's findings: the deceased had been shot, and they'd died before the fire broke out; no smoke or carbon dioxide was in their lungs. Evidently it was a case of murder, but the sheriff asked the doctor not to say anything until he had finished his investigation.

A slightly tragic aspect to the case was added by the doctor's announcement that the woman had been pregnant: it was another instance of the couple's indefensible irresponsibility that they hadn't bothered to ensure the baby's legal rights by giving birth to it within the bonds of matrimony.

The sheriff released to the local newspaper a sketchy statement in which he informed them that a fire had broken out in the Communists' home and that they'd perished. There was no question of crime, but alcohol may have played a part. This wasn't a complete fabrication, for the sheriff had found a bottle of household alcohol that the murderer (the sheriff used the word reluctantly, since he couldn't find a better one) had presumably used when he'd set fire to the place.

Now it was a question of finding out who the guilty party was. The sheriff knew everyone in the county personally, and he was convinced that all of them were righteous enough to kill a traitor who wanted to sell the country to the Russians. Obviously they would only do it under extreme circumstances, however, because they all belonged to the Finland-Soviet Friendship Society, an organization dedicated to the principle that bygones were bygones even out here near the border. No, it must have been a question of provocation.

The sheriff tried to figure out what sort of provocation would legitimate the perpetrator's (or perpetrators'?) action, but to his regret he couldn't come up with any. So he decided to try to demonstrate that the deceased had been spies in the service of a foreign power. But once again he couldn't think of anything in the area that might be considered of interest to a foreign power. During the last days of the war the front lines had been close by, due east of Tuokojärvi, but now wasn't anything there but marsh and forest.

For a while the sheriff tried to suggest that the district medical examiner describe the case as double suicide. The young couple had taken their own lives when, in the healthy country atmosphere, they'd seen the error of their ways. The district medical examiner thought they might have a hard time proving that they had shot themselves when the weapon was nowhere to be found and they'd burned down the cabin after they were dead. The doctor's objections surprised the sheriff, who'd thought of his colleague as a patriotically minded person. Well, when he eventually found the perpetrators the doctor would of course write a statement saying that the cause of the crime was temporary insanity. The sheriff had another reason to lament the new social welfare laws that had eliminated the village idiots and paupers whom one used to see before the war camping out in the pigsties of affluent farms. One of them would have served quite nicely now. It wouldn't have been hard to get him to confess, and a few years in the house of correction would have felt like pure vacation. But as things stood now, the sheriff was afraid that he might have to send the guilty party to prison. And if he took too long finding him, it would reflect on his abilities as sheriff; in this postwar world, politics were mixed up with crime, and justice did the work of scoundrels.

Depressed, the sheriff returned to the scene of the crime, sat down on a rock, and brooded. It was a harder problem than any one Sherlock Holmes or Hercule Poirot had had to face; he had to catch a murderer and then prove him innocent. At that moment he saw something that made his eyes open wide in amazement. A soldier in complete combat uniform was approaching the remaining outbuildings on the other side of the glade. The soldier hadn't seen him, and instinctively the sheriff took cover behind a rock even though he could see that the soldier was one of their own. Moreover, he remembered that the war had been over for six years, and he began to wonder if it was an hallucination caused by the stark chimney standing in the middle of the foundation of the ruined house. Inevitably his thoughts wandered back to the war and to places like Poventsa, Petroskoi and Karhumäki which he had helped destroy as a company captain.[25] The soldier who had just looked into the empty barn could have been one of his men, but he wasn't; on his arm was the triangle of the Yellow Brigade. He was the perpetrator returning to the scene of the crime according to the universal laws of the whodunnit.

Actually, Viktor Käppärä was just checking to see if there might be any flour or potatoes in the outbuildings; he'd been so scared the first time that he'd forgot to check. The sheriff never doubted for a moment that he'd found the perpetrator. He heaved a sigh of relief that it wasn't one of the local people. He slipped the safety off his service revolver, but something stopped him from arresting the man: he called it intuition (the three authors later changed it to "God's will"). Like the deceased, he also thought Viktor was a deserter or a draft-dodger who hadn't dared show himself for fear of reprisals; it was also possible that he'd committed other crimes that forced him to stay in hiding. But it seemed totally incredible that he'd lived by himself in the forest for so many years, and so the sheriff decided to follow him to see if he could catch the whole gang. He was pleased that he'd finally found a new bank in which to deposit all previously unsolved crimes.

From the barn Viktor went to the storehouse; he could see that the infiltrator had been telling the truth when he'd said that all they had was the bread they were eating. In a lumber room he found a few potatoes, put them in a sack, and flung the sack on his back. He was disappointed, but he would have been more so if he'd seen that the Enemy had been living lavishly while he'd had to live by his wits. Then he headed back to his post.

The sheriff followed a good distance behind. The soldier went down to the beach and followed it to the other side of the lake. Then he suddenly turned inland, climbed a hill, and disappeared among the trees. In the reeds the sheriff found a rowboat with a lot of fishing equipment, which confirmed that the draft-dodgers had been living there quite a while. Their hideout must not be far away. With his pistol cocked, he crawled on his stomach up the hill; obviously the men were desperate and dangerous.

On the top of the rise he was surprised again. From the potato cellar a trench ran to a little bunker with wood-supported walls and a firing embrasure. A periscope was in the bunker, and on a ledge lay a flare gun and a couple of grenades.

**A moment later** the soldier left his bunker and went to his post, rifle in hand. Completely routinely, he scanned the terrain in front of the embankment with his periscope, then looked up at the sky in all directions; after he finished he began to whittle absently on a stick. What the sheriff saw before him was a sentry at the front who had just relieved a nonexistent comrade. The door to the potato cellar was open; it was easy to see that it was empty. An automatic pistol was leaning against the wall, and a couple of clips were lying on a shelf.

The Yellow Brigade had been stationed in this section of the front at the end of the war. This man was wearing the insignia of the Yellow Brigade on his arm. When he'd gone on watch, he'd put on his steel helmet just the way soldiers had been instructed to. Only the impossible seemed possible: that this soldier was single-handedly continuing World War II. (Even as the sheriff thought this thought, he changed "World War II" to "War of Continuation" since Finland's war was a separate and just war that merely happened to be fought on the wrong side.) Because of some accident or mistake he'd been left behind in the woods. The dedication, the loyalty moved the sheriff to tears. If the whole Finnish army had been like this man, Karelia might still be free and the border might be at Lake Onega![26] At home the sheriff kept a bottle of water from Onega on his mantlepiece.

How could he arrest this hero for murder? The sheriff's heart bled at the thought that the man would be forced to ruin everything he held holy; he'd have to sully the honor of the Finnish soldier. Why did *he* have to be the one?

Then the sheriff pulled himself together.

He simply *couldn't* arrest the soldier for murder. If it got out that a soldier in the Finnish army had executed two Communists, the repercussions could be enormous; it'd be a bigger scandal than the business with the weapon caches.[27] If he arrested the man, he'd risk the nation's security and independence, which he had no authority to do. Relieved, the sheriff realized that now the incident had grown from a local crime to an issue of international politics in which murder and arson took on a completely different character from ordinary circumstances. The investigation of the matter wasn't his affair any longer. But he did have to decide on his own (a patriotic decision, of course) to keep the whole thing secret. He couldn't arrest the soldier, but he couldn't go up to him and tell him that the war was over, either; in both cases the crime would have been revealed.

Still, the matter wasn't settled. As long as the district medical examiner wouldn't agree to write a death certificate for double suicide it was the sheriff's duty to find a guilty party, and now that he knew who it was, the task was even more impossible. He decided to tell the doctor everything and appeal to his patriotism.

The man must be mad! said the doctor when he heard the sheriff's story.

The sheriff blew up and asked how loyalty and discipline could be madness. The soldier was only doing his duty; how could that be mad? He wasn't doing anything that the whole Finnish army hadn't done for four years. If the soldier by the lake in the woods was mad, the whole Finnish army had been mad! The *whole war* had been one big mistake, and all the victims had died in vain and Risto Ryti and Väinö Tanner[28] and Mannerheim had been misguided nincompoops when they'd tried to preserve Finland's independence. Certainly the doctor wasn't implying that, was he?

The district medical examiner had served in the War of Liberation (he always called it the War of Liberation instead of the Civil War; the Whites had liberated the Reds —against their will, of course, but in their own best interests), and he'd never doubted that it was a just war. He had never doubted the legitimacy of the Winter War or the War of Continuation either; as long as they were winning, he'd applauded enthusiastically.

But, as a doctor, over the years he'd developed a skeptical streak, and when the Germans began to fare badly he grew critical of them. After El Alamein he'd lost all his faith in victory. (In the nation's more enlightened circles, people could be divided into two factions: those who saw after El Alamein that the war was lost, and those who didn't. Of course the insight required no action; it was enough that one could prove that one shook one's head at the time and mumbled "Now it's over" or "Our goose is cooked" or "It's all going to hell" to be regarded as an astute realist. These realists later became the core group behind President Paasikivi's *realpolitik* in dealing with our large neighbor to the East,[29] whose geographical position was God's blunder for which the Finns couldn't be held responsible for.) After Stalingrad, the district medical examiner's opinion of Adolph Hitler deteriorated considerably, and he began to think that Hitler wasn't quite right in the head. When, in the last phase of the war, President

Ryti signed the Ribbentrop Pact,[30] he began to think that Ryti wasn't quite right in the head, either. So when Ryti was thrown in the clink with Väinö Tanner after the war,[31] the district medical examiner didn't think any great injustice had been done; as far as he was concerned, it should have been done five years earlier. But since he had no admiration for hindsight, he never mentioned it to anyone.

However, he *had* had a hard time swallowing the Germans' setting fire to Lapland.[32] Unlike most of his colleagues, he couldn't justify it by saying that the Finns, as their comrades-in-arms, had let the Germans down. If one believed that the Finns had betrayed the Germans, one would also, thought the doctor, have to share the Germans' responsibility for all the crimes (that's what he called them) they'd committed. Though the doctor wasn't especially fond of Jews, when he heard that they'd gassed six million he was shocked: that was nearly double the population of Finland. Of course the Finns weren't Jews, but the Finno-Ugrian race wasn't Aryan either. And perhaps it wouldn't have been too long before Hitler discovered that they had immigrated to Finland at some point from the banks of the Volga and therefore ought to be eradicated. (Even Paavo Nurmi had small, squinty eyes and prominent cheekbones, which revealed his Slavic roots even though Wäinö Aaltonen, the country's greatest sculptor, depicted him as an ancient Olympic champion of purest pedigree.)[33] And so the doctor came to the paradoxical conclusion that the country had preserved its independence both by fighting for it and by losing the war instead of winning it.

Therefore, he said no. He couldn't be party to a false

death certificate protecting a murderer. He wasn't interested in the argument that what was done in wartime was actually bravery, not murder; stubbornly he pointed out that the war was over and it was no excuse that the soldier didn't know it. (Once the doctor had gone to town, parked in the wrong place, and had to pay the ticket even though he could prove that the street had got No Parking restrictions since his last visit.) Law and justice had to prevail, his record was spotless, and he had no intention (just before his approaching retirement) of sullying his Honor by being party to a criminal act. At this point—though it was repugnant to him—the sheriff threatened to ask for an audit of the doctor's income tax returns (this was before the system of obligatory receipts, when the medical profession was still a calling): the district medical examiner relented and wrote out the death certificate.

In this manner Viktor Käppärä was relieved of two murders without in any way being relieved of his guilty conscience.

**After this incident** followed the long silence that Käp-pärä's biographers have compared to Mao's Long March. The forgotten soldier wasn't heard from again for twenty-five years. More precisely, the sheriff made sure that nothing was heard from him.

However, the number of unsolved crimes in the sheriff's district increased alarmingly. Hunters committed suicide in the woods or were killed accidentally, and campers were robbed at night and food was stolen from remote farms. It wasn't at all certain that Viktor committed all these dastardly crimes (perhaps he didn't commit any of them), but the sheriff never dared to investigate for fear that they might prove that the solitary soldier had struck again. And if that were so, it would have increased the sheriff's own guilt as an accessory to the crimes, and further sullied his Honor as a civil servant.

Also, the political responsibility of his decision already weighed heavily on his conscience. He started drinking to forget at least temporarily that the country's future as an independent nation rested on his shoulders alone. The more he pondered the issue, the more fearful the political consequences became. Of course it's possible that, driven by guilt, he unconsciously enlarged them to justify what he had done.

But even if the sheriff didn't do much to capture lawbreakers, he did do his best to prevent crime. He took frequent trips to the woods (which took their toll on his liquor-ravaged body) and placed packets of provisions where the soldier couldn't miss them. As long as the solitary soldier had everything he needed, reasoned the sheriff, he wouldn't stray from his post, so he tried to figure out exactly what the soldier would need. It isn't so easy figuring out what a person needs if he doesn't tell you; the sheriff suddenly found himself in the same position as an industrial magnate who has to figure out the lowest salary he can get away with offering his workers.

The sheriff was rather clever at keeping Viktor at his post. For wrapping paper, he carefully chose parts of newspapers with appropriate war news. Actually it was very easy to find appropriate newspapers; the more time passed after the war ended, the more the newspapers talked about war and the less about peace. In this way Viktor got the impression that the fronts surged back and forth: one moment the Russians took Budapest and Prague, the next, violent battles raged in Greece and Palestine—while in darkest Africa they were fighting everywhere. The constant talk of the Cold War must have seemed odd in light of all these jungle wars, but the sheriff assumed quite correctly that the sentry would think it had to do with his own war in the north, which apparently had developed into some sort of stalemate. The fact of the matter was that never before had there been so much fighting as after World War II. It certainly didn't seem excessive for Finland to have at least *one* man participating.

What really worried the sheriff was that he couldn't quite depend on the district medical examiner to keep his mouth shut. After his retirement, he'd grown quite senile and babbled all the time. Luckily, most of what he said was completely disregarded and no one believed his stories even though as long as he lived no one questioned his diagnoses and prescriptions, which made him much more dangerous in his office than the soldier in the woods. But a doctor has the right to put a person to death as long as he does it through ignorance or a mistake, while a soldier has only his orders to fall back on. And there were various times during the Long Silence when sympathy for Käppärä's loyalty to duty wouldn't have been terribly strong.

The sixties, for instance, were a bad time for heroes. A wind from the Left blew over all of Europe, and Old World values were questioned relentlessly. Students and workers protested against imperialism, militarism, and oppression, and violence had to go into underground torture chambers or up in skyscrapers, into the board rooms of multinational corporations. Like driftwood, Finland followed the current and, led by the director of the radio,[34] youth attacked everything in the nation that was held precious and holy. They reviled the memory of Mannerheim and the reputation of the Americans in Vietnam; they questioned the right to tear down old buildings and wrote ballads against the banks and the Establishment. And it didn't seem totally impossible that behind them all stood the President himself, who, as he grew older, grew more progressive and more unwilling to retire. He was as stubborn as Viktor himself, and perhaps he might not have been pleased if a competitor in perseverance had turned up.

Thus, the sheriff had reason to be uneasy; and the relief he felt when the district medical examiner finally died would have turned to terror if he'd suspected that the doctor had written a sort of confession so that he could meet his Maker (who knew so much about sin but so little about medicine) with a clearer conscience. In Finland people often have an unquestioning belief in the written word, whether it's written by a madman or Poet Laureate; and no matter how senile the doctor was no one would have doubted the veracity of his posthumous papers even though he couldn't remember he'd written them ten minutes after he'd finished and sealed them in an envelope marked "I confess" (in the spirit of Zola's "J'accuse").

In time the papers were found between the pages of a book about Otto Ville Kuusinen as a Romantic,[35] and when the political wind of the seventies shifted to the Right and the director of the radio got the boot and only the President remained a radical, one could regard the doctor's disclosures as Leftist propaganda, which made them as worthless as Truth. The biographers dismissed them as "a spiteful old man's attack against the society that had embittered him." With this choice of words they succeeded in making it sound as though it were all the fault of Kuusinen and socialism—which is, after all, just a Romantic dream. They went on to use almost one hundred pages to extol the qualities that Käppärä developed during his long solitude, his long silence—the heroic years. What they lacked in information, they filled in with Robinson Crusoe and a number of writings by holy men in India who'd sat meditating for very long periods alone in the Himalayas.

Viktor continued writing to his mother right up to his death and fifteen years after hers. When he had obviously given up hope of ever mailing them, they gradually changed and became more like diary notes. He began all the letters with "Dear Mama," but what followed didn't seem intended for his mother, if indeed for anyone at all.

*Dear Mama,*

*I've thought about it a lot and I think even though I did the right thing for Lisa not to fuck her that time, I did the wrong thing for myself. How do you think it feels to die with your cherry intact?*

That was a whole letter, and it wasn't even signed. Obviously, by writing it down Viktor was trying to work through a painful moral problem. Was it possible to do the right thing for oneself and those closest to you at the same time? Wasn't injustice built into love?

The three authors plunged into this letter with delight.

They (the priest) emphasized what a miracle it was that Viktor had lived as spotless a life as a saint's, and that his only bride was the Battle for the True Cause (they didn't specify what that Cause was). Even though Viktor sometimes doubted his choice, Christ had also battled with Himself—and, as the priest asserted, cleanliness is arrived at only by cleansing oneself of dirt, not by denying its existence.

In Viktor's bunker, they found a bra that was as hard and stiff as if it had just been starched; the starch proved to be sperm. In the two cloth cups were the collected decades of yearning for love. The biographers declined to mention the garment. Yet it did worry the sheriff, who was afraid that behind the bra was another unsolved crime. Apparently it made no difference to Viktor whether he killed men or women.

This thought also crossed the mind of the psychiatrist,

who'd noticed that Viktor's birthday fell on the same day as Henri Désiré Landru's execution;[36] this couldn't be just coincidence. Right away he saw the possibilities for a major paper on the destructive effects of enforced abstinence on sexual morality. In the absence of emotional contact between human beings, according to his theory, constantly overheated fantasies bring about a state of impotence that finds no other outlet than murder when the opportunity presents itself. He was convinced (and the sheriff was afraid) that further investigation would reveal several more murdered women in the Sevettilä district. But this work (which would make him famous) had to be deferred until Käppärä was firmly installed in the pantheon of Finnish heroes. Of course he didn't breathe a word of these plans to his author-colleagues.

"I've discovered that I'm the most powerful being in the world," Viktor wrote. "When I wander through the forest, all the animals run away. The rabbit leaps into the bushes, the grouse flies off with a crash, the fox slinks away, the wolf runs like a whipped dog, and even the bear turns and trots off when we meet. Only the mosquitoes attack me. I can kill hundreds of them, but they keep attacking and I can see that my blood is more valuable to them than their own lives. Even so, I can't get myself to admire their courage."

The team of authors passed over the supreme irony in Viktor's reflections and maintained that his belief that he was invincible in the woods (i.e., Finland) was because he was defending his country. The mosquitoes represented the Enemy, as numberless as they were unconscious, who lusted after Christian (Topelius's) blood but who never succeeded in vanquishing the Brave One who stood like a

northern Rock of Gibraltar transformed into flesh and blood.[37] (Off the record, the lawyer pointed out that the sheriff had demonstrated his incompetence by failing to provide bug spray when he knew how many mosquitoes and gnats were in the marshes.)

Without knowing it, Viktor commented on the sheriff's action, too. He thought that the sheriff's packets were from the Enemy, who had dropped them for the infiltrators he'd liquidated. He wrote that it was repulsive for him to eat something that came from cans bearing a Soviet red star even though he liked crabs from Kamchatka and sturgeon from the Volga. Luckily, he never found out that the nickel content of the fish exceeded the limits that the health authorities considered safe. (Of course they subsequently raised them to a politically acceptable level.)

Otherwise, Viktor became more and more restrained in his depiction of external events. Most of his writing became a sort of philosophizing that gradually turned into a list of worries about all sorts of ailments. For example, it wasn't at all clear if he killed any more Enemies, even though we do have proof that he killed one person and fought with many others. The only place some hint occurs is in a letter where he says that he'll no longer kill anything except what he can eat.

And he couldn't eat journalists even if he'd known that a reporter's intention was to get an uncritical public to swallow *him* in one big gulp.

**Without a free press** the free are not free and the oppressed don't know that they're oppressed. It's hard to know which is better: that Nixon was exposed as a scoundrel or that Stalin wasn't. At any rate, that someone with a secret can never be careful enough with the press was an axiom that the sheriff hadn't learned in his remote corner of the country. An indiscreet remark threw over all his plans and became the cause of unhappiness and death, which are the basic ingredients for the creation of a hero.

At the opening of the Wagon Wheel Inn (later the Viktor Käppärä Motel) the sheriff presided at the journalists' table. Finally modern times had come to Sevettilä: to prevent young people from moving away, the county fathers had decided to encourage tourism, thereby providing jobs in the service industry.

It should come as no surprise that the sheriff had opposed plans for strangers to prowl around in the woods. He talked about the pollution of Nature and moral decay, but nothing helped; the motel was built. The only chance the sheriff saw was, through the press, to scare the public from going out into the woods where Viktor lived. So he informed them that in the last phase of the war the fighting had raged in the county's eastern sector and that because of the danger of land mines it wasn't advisable to go there.

Among the reporters dispatched to the scene (who availed themselves of vast quantities of free cognac) there were as always a few Stalinist youths who couldn't pass up an occasion to besmirch the honor of the Finnish army and extol the Enemy's courage and prowess. It was true in this instance, too: a brash, shaggy fellow dressed in an American army surplus jacket said disdainfully that the Finnish army had done more running than fighting. That burned the sheriff (who had plenty of kindling inside him), and he replied that the Finns hadn't given an inch and that at this very moment there was one man still at his post.

As soon as he'd said it he wanted to bite his tongue.

The long-haired Stalinist (actually from the country's most conservative newspaper) immediately asked him if it was true; the sheriff said of course it wasn't. The reporter asked if the sheriff was in the habit of lying and the sheriff replied that he never lied and that there was a ghost in the woods, a soldier who'd come back from the dead. He was headless and had scary green eyes that glowed in the dark; the district medical examiner had seen him. The reporter asked to speak with the district medical examiner and the sheriff said that he was dead and thought that with this brilliant stroke he'd gotten out of a very tight spot.

But the journalist, who was bored to death writing accounts of the openings of remote hotels, decided to write a sensationalistic story about the Ghost of the Border. He could use the sheriff's story as a starting point and make up the rest; he'd just go for a little walk in the woods to add some local color. A military ghost was something new; and as far as he was concerned, a ghost was just about what the country needed to defend it.

The wonderful thing about ghosts is that they're as unpredictable and difficult to track down as the Loch Ness monster; they appear only when they feel like it and to whom they like. He'd make the country (and himself) famous, and afterward he'd write a ballad about the soldier who'd shot one of the Enemy who had begged for mercy on his knees; as soon as he'd killed the Enemy, the soldier was hit by a bullet and since he'd never had time to atone for his evil deed, he'd had to stay at his post forever, waiting to be relieved.

It was absolutely brilliant, thought the reporter, who'd been a substitute theater critic for a while and had developed a flair for the dramatic. An ambitious journalist, he would gladly have exposed the President himself just as his colleagues on the *Washington Post* had done—if it hadn't been against the law in Finland. A former publicist had resurrected the remains of socialism and become the general director of the radio because of it;[38] who knows what he'd become with the ghost of militarism in tow?

And so the journalist fell asleep with the anticipation and joy of the optimistic young. For the sheriff, however, alcohol wasn't a good tranquilizer any longer; he tossed and turned in his bed, plagued by terrible dreams in which the soldier pursued him with a fixed bayonet.

**For a change,** there is a lively and skilled description of what happened when the journalist met the solitary soldier. Of course Käppärä's biographers refused to place any credence in it. Their reasoning came out of the relatively accurate observation that the journalist and Viktor couldn't communicate in a mutually comprehensible way because one was in World War II and the other in the seventies: there are myriads of examples of how a blameless person's wartime acts and statements become distorted by snot-nosed investigators and other sensation-mongers more concerned with filthy lucre than with their country. The only thing the authors conceded was that the reporter possibly did meet Käppärä, which was more than anyone else had done when the article was published. Of course the article was turned down by the conservative paper the reporter was employed by, and he had to offer it to a particularly sleazy magazine that published pictures of the man with the smallest cock in the country and things of that ilk. The worst of it all was that the article had no photographs to substantiate it; not many people believed the story that Käppärä had seized the reporter's camera. Consequently, the reporter made hardly anything from the article—which showed that not even the magazine's editor believed it was true.

The journalist was terribly disappointed; he had almost

lost his life to get the story. When he subsequently did lose it, it comforted him very little to know that this time he'd been taken seriously.

The reporter couldn't help drawing analogies between his meeting with Käppärä and Stanley's meeting with Livingstone. Unfortunately, it wasn't as cordial as the noble explorers' confrontation had been. (By the way, on his trek Stanley had had to liquidate a few dozen surly blacks who hadn't learned to mind their manners.) When the journalist reached out *his* hand, he got the barrel of a rifle stuck in his stomach. This was no way to treat a rescuer, he thought.

But it was obvious that Viktor didn't regard him as an angel of mercy carrying a message of peace and brotherhood. Instead, what he saw was a long-haired, scruffy man in an American uniform with a sergeant's stripes on his arm. In addition, on his chest it said "U.S. Air Force," which made it easy to see that he'd been dropped from a plane. America was an ally of Russia. In short, he saw an Enemy.

No one *wants* to see the Enemy; there are always problems about what to do with him. The simplest thing is to shoot him, and that was Viktor's first inclination, too. But in the same moment he was overwhelmed by a strong urge to talk to someone and he couldn't resist exchanging a few words with the infiltrator before he "put him out of his misery." (Viktor had gotten the phrase from a detective novel and liked it because it seemed to make killing into a humane act.) The journalist claimed that he'd gotten lost. It was true; he was in such bad shape that all his body could take was a very short hike in the woods to sop up local color. But apparently he'd lost his bearings and headed in the wrong direction, and then he'd wandered around

in the marshes for hours before arriving at the shore of the lake. And he hadn't had even a single beer to fortify himself with.

Viktor wasn't sympathetic. Furthermore, he didn't believe a word of what the American sergeant was saying. Even less because he spoke Finnish, which proved that he was a spy and saboteur. He said that it was obvious that the sergeant had been sent to destroy the outpost.

How am I supposed to do that with a camera? asked the journalist. That was when Viktor took the camera and threw it far away. Then he put a bullet in it, but it didn't explode. The journalist could have cried, but he was afraid to: he'd much rather have met a ghost than this armed madman.

He tried asking the sentry if he might by any chance happen to know that the war was over.

Viktor wondered why in that case he was wearing a uniform.

The journalist said that he'd bought it in a boutique.

Booteek? said Viktor.

Boutique, the journalist said, thereby conclusively revealing his foreign origin.

The war ended thirty years ago, said the journalist. Viktor laughed right in his face and asked if he thought that Finnish soldiers were born yesterday: he'd read the papers enough to know that the Russians had invaded both Budapest and Prague, and there was fighting in Asia, the Middle East, and South America. Instead of ending, it was obvious that it had only recently become a *real* World War!

The journalist explained that these were new wars.

Viktor asked what happened to the old war.

The Allies won, said the journalist.

That means the Russians won, said Viktor.

The journalist said that they had.

Viktor laughed and asked how it was then that he hadn't seen any Russians. As far as he could tell, they were on their last legs if they had to send American soldiers instead of their own.

The journalist said that the Americans and Russians were enemies.

Viktor said that he thought the Germans and Americans were enemies. The journalist said they were allies, and that all of them were fascist imperialist pigs.

Then the Germans must have won, said Viktor, and the journalist said that the Germans and Italians and Japanese had lost and were all American allies now.

What about England and France? asked Viktor.

They won, too, but both England and France lost their colonies and weren't powerful any longer.

Viktor was terribly amused by the American's crazy talk. Everything he said pointed to a complete German victory, but the fact that the Americans had dropped the sergeant in was the best proof that the war was not over. No, the American was obviously a cunning liar.

Viktor knew how dangerous it was to give in to his personal feelings in war, but he couldn't stop himself from saying that it really went against his grain to shoot such an excellent liar. However, since he was the only person stationed there he couldn't very well take prisoners of war; he couldn't comply with even the minimum standards of the Geneva Convention, and he didn't want to be the cause of Finland's military being accused of inhumane treatment of prisoners of war.

Frightened, the journalist asked if that meant that Viktor would shoot a fellow human being.

One can read Viktor's reply in the journalist's article:

" 'I was in basic training for three months before I was sent to the front,' said the soldier. 'That was where I learned how to kill people. We began by shooting at cardboard silhouettes. The more we hit the silhouettes, the higher scores we got. If you think it's different when you use people instead of silhouettes, you're wrong. The people *become* silhouettes. I've never killed anything but silhouettes.'

" 'But *I'm* not a silhouette,' I told him. 'I can talk and I'm scared; I'm on my knees pleading for my life.'

" 'Yes,' said the soldier. 'I know that I shouldn't fraternize with the Enemy. It really makes it harder to see them as Enemies. That's why Enemies usually speak a foreign language, and that's why the Russians make such wonderful ones; you can't understand a word they're saying. But this business of infiltrators speaking Finnish is a problem; that's probably why they're considered criminals instead of Enemies. Unfortunately, they're the only kind I've had to deal with recently. It's possible that they're Finnish deserters and it's horrible to shoot your own countrymen, but it's easier when you think of them as silhouettes. Also, the real goal of war is to kill people—that's the whole point. But it isn't my job to define the goal of war; my job is to follow orders. And I'll do just that until Sergeant Hurmalainen comes back and gives me an order to do something else.'

"I asked the soldier where the sergeant was, and he said he'd gone back to the main troop and hadn't been heard from since. That was when our troops launched a new offensive, most likely in the fall of '44.

"I realized that it was pointless to count on the sergeant coming to my rescue, so I swore to the soldier that I wasn't a traitor—I was a Finn.

" 'American-Finn,' he said, adding that his mother had been in America, too. He told me how she'd worked as a chambermaid for J. P. Morgan and come back home with a pancake skillet. I told him that was a funny coincidence because my grandfather had been one of Morgan's gardeners. He might have known the soldier's mother—what was her name? 'Käppärä,' he said, and then he said that her maiden name was Hamberg. Lydia Hamberg. I asked if she had a turned-up nose, blond hair, and little slanty-squinty eyes like her son and he said that described her to a T. Then I said that I'd seen a photo of Morgan's servants on Grandpa's mantlepiece in which a girl like that was standing in a white apron next to him. Could it be her?

"Käppärä asked if there were many Communists in America, and I swore that you get kicked out of the army if you're a Communist.

"Then he said that he was going to let me go even though he knew it was a mistake, but he couldn't shoot a man whose grandfather had been a servant in J. P. Morgan's house with his mother."

That was basically the essence of the article. What followed were long, almost Runebergian tirades about Käppärä's incredible military achievements, which were unsurpassed in the whole world. It wasn't only because Viktor had spared his life that the journalist wrote what he wrote; as a lover of all Finnish records, he was moved by the pure patriotic fervor that sweeps the country during a national sports match—and which swept his Stalinism away in one fell swoop. And so when he was fired from his newspaper for having made fun of a Finnish soldier, thereby casting the country's armed forces in a bad light, he felt both maligned and enraged: they'd got it all wrong.

**It wasn't hard** for Käppärä's biographers to catch the journalist in a lie. The whole section that dealt with how it felt to kill people was obviously swiped from an interview Lt. William Calley had given to an American newspaper the same day he was released from house arrest for having murdered twenty-two civilians in Vietnam. He'd been convicted of twenty-two murders, but he said he'd only killed five. In any case, all the inhabitants of the village of My Lai had been killed and it wasn't really clear who did what except that a little over one hundred women, children, and old people died, and Lt. Calley had been the officer in charge.

He'd had orders to destroy the village, and destroy it he had. In the past the Americans had destroyed many villages the same way without causing any commotion. But then someone came along and took pictures of all the victims and all of a sudden some Nervous Nellies got upset by the sight of dead children clinging to their dead mothers. So a guilty party had to be found, and they picked good old Lt. Rusty Calley. They wrote songs about Rusty and he became a national hero, and writer John Stack got $100,000 for writing his life story. He wouldn't have gotten $10 for writing the life stories of all the victims; poor, yellow-skinned people don't have life stories.

It was Rusty, not Viktor, who said that shooting people was just like shooting silhouettes. On the contrary: Viktor

had written in his letter to his Mama that he couldn't sleep after taking the lives of the two infiltrators.

Here the authors talk about the sensibility of the Finnish fighting man—that it is nobler to kill if it gives no sense of pleasure—but they concede that extra difficulties were added by the fact that the victims spoke Finnish and weren't in uniform. At this point they refer to the enormous trials the previous generation suffered in the Civil War when Finns had to kill Finns. It was during this period that the Reds began to be regarded as foreigners, and from this attitude stems the feeling that all political shades left of center are still not considered patriotic—or at least reliable. Curiously enough, the Left never accuses the Right of being unpatriotic in spite of their collaboration with the Germans. For in Finland sympathizing with Germany has always been synonymous with patriotism. When the Germans burned Lapland, it was a test of patriotism, and those who thereafter remained friendly to Germany were regarded as the most stalwart of patriots. The secret police never felt the need to put *them* on their list of suspicious elements.

By the way, it would be extremely shortsighted to make fun of the country's secret police; by no means do they sit idly by or concern themselves merely with writing down names of Left-wing sympathizers. As soon as they learned Käppärä's name, they assigned two men to collect information on him. It wasn't hard to find out that he'd been reported missing on the last day of the war and hadn't been heard from since. He hadn't been reported dead, and he hadn't returned from a prisoner-of-war camp. Also, it turned out that the article was quite correct that he'd been stationed in Sevetillä when the armistice began. So it was possible—if one disregards the fact that it was impossible—that he actually was still at his post in the forest.

If that was the case, the problem was to figure out what to do with him. The secret police aren't empowered to look for missing persons the way ordinary police are; more often it's a question of seeing that they stay properly (and permanently) missing. They contacted the sheriff in Sevettilä; he didn't need much coaxing before all was revealed. When the truth finally came out, they had to figure out how to bury it again: for the sheriff had to acknowledge the murder of the two Communists, and he couldn't deny that he also suspected Käppärä of most of the other unsolved crimes as well. He hadn't wanted to investigate them for fear of further incriminating the soldier who, in the sheriff's eyes, was a hero.

The secret police have no heroes—only useful and useless persons—and they couldn't help feeling that the sheriff had acted very wisely in keeping Käppärä under wraps. At the time, the murder of the Communists could undoubtedly have caused an international incident. Now, of course, the picture had changed; there were so many different kinds of Communists in the world that once in a while it might be an act of mercy to liquidate a few. But of course it wasn't easy for a layman to know who is liquidatable and who isn't. Off the top of their heads, the secret police couldn't say whether the victims had been Stalinists, revisionists, or Maoists, and under no circumstances did they feel that the sheriff should have disposed of Käppärä. It was possible at the present moment that the solitary soldier might be useful to them: military exploits were needed to counterbalance all the peace conferences and disarmament talks, and Käppärä's madness might just turn out to give the nation's "defense spirit" a big boost. (This so-called defense spirit is a phenomenon completely independent of disarmament, friendship pacts, peace treaties, agreement over national borders, and respect for other nations' sovereignty; it's a delicate seedling that, with proper care, can thrive in even the most peaceful soil until it bears fruit in the form of missiles, tanks, and all-weather pursuit planes.)

After World War I, a German general said, "Aber einen Feind muss man ja haben"[39]—every country needs an Enemy. Nowadays countries have to build up their armaments without (acknowledged) Enemies; there's no need of heroes either.

Viktor Käppärä had turned up at just the right moment.

The Minister of the Interior was informed of the contents of the intelligence agency's report. He was fully aware that Käppärä fell under the jurisdiction of the Ministry of Defense, but he was afraid of his falling into the hands of the armed forces, whom one couldn't depend on in sensitive security matters. In industrialized countries the generals hadn't been able to keep up with political developments; they no longer had any more importance than locomotive engineers who transport iron ingots to steel mills where they're later turned into weapons. No one listened any longer to the officers' unrealistic speculations in security matters about which, despite all their best intentions, they couldn't know anything since they hadn't been informed as to what the superpowers had agreed on concerning the outcome of planned local wars. In underdeveloped countries, of course, the situation was slightly different. There the generals were paid bonuses according to the amount of weaponry used, and thus it was cost-effective to give them power. If they didn't actually initiate war with their neighbors, one could depend on a coup by a corrupt general, and the further consumption of war matériel was assured.

Of course the Minister of the Interior should have informed the President,[40] but after having taken several dozen trips to the U.S.S.R., where he'd gone hunting and fishing with the boys in the Politburo, the President wasn't completely reliable either. The fact was that one never knew *where* his sympathies lay. After the tragic explosions in the gunpowder factory in Lapua, it was thought that he might insist that cartridges be purchased abroad where they're filled by machine instead of by women's hands.[41] But part of the success of Finnish wars depended no doubt on the fact that gunpowder was stuffed so lovingly into shells, that female labor was so cheap, and that it didn't run dry even though every once in a while fifty women were pulverized in an unfortunate explosion. Besides, the risk of explosion is nonexistent, stated a highly placed military officer immediately after the accident, adding that he himself would work at such a job any time if he weren't needed for other duties in the service of his country. Such poorly timed platitudes damaged the image of the military, and thus it was best that they didn't get a chance to open their mouths except to bark out orders whose basic rationality no one checked.

In this case, the President, who had been a sergeant in the army,[42] contented himself with offering his condolences to all the motherless children (Mannerheim had done the opposite) and let the captains of industry build a new gunpowder factory where fifty new women began stuffing shells with gunpowder as lovingly as before. This not only supported defense (where women ought to have their rightful place) but also earned much-needed cash for the country. Some of the ammunition was exported to South Africa and Rhodesia, which paid handsomely for Finnish-made hunting rifles. Marksmanship was in fact the only sport whites could practice with the country's black majority, and the hunting season had been extended to include the whole year.

It was clear, then, that industry needed Viktor most. The real question was how to market him: the way the nation had done with Sibelius (Finlandia vodka)? Mannerheim (Karjala beer)? Or our Olympic gold medalists, who sold everything from Japanese track shoes to Canadian skis? Käppärä could become the symbol of perseverance, reliability, and tenacity, qualities that suited both the shipping and automotive industries. To say nothing of what he might mean to the shaping of future defense budgets.

The Minister of the Interior faced a difficult decision: to whom should the sentry be assigned? Then he thought of the advertising agencies; they were the experts at exploitation. And not every minister can count on being appointed as an ambassador or a provincial governor; it couldn't hurt to have a multinational advertising agency in your debt. It was only a question of figuring out which agency represented the CIA in Finland—which wasn't as easy as one might think because all of them seemed to.

Of course the simplest way would be to give the case to the courts. But what did the courts know about the interests of the country? And who should be prosecuted— Private Käppärä (who'd been declared dead) or the Finnish army? He was the last remnant of the Finnish army fighting World War II, and if he were found guilty of killing two Communists, there would be no limits to all the lawsuits they could expect. And how do you punish an entire army? An army can't be punished, only defeated—

and therefore, conversely, a victorious army is always innocent.

For history has shown that it was always the vanquished army that committed the crimes.

When the Minister of the Interior realized that Viktor Käppärä was irrefutable proof that Finland had not been defeated, he jumped out of his chair with happiness. This meant that the war crimes trials were unjustified and the war claims reparations could be rescinded!

But when he saw that, in spite of Käppärä, the country didn't have the resources to go about reclaiming all its money, he grew depressed: there was nothing to do but to get whatever advertising value they could squeeze out of the guy. The Minister called up a multinational consulting firm and asked the vice-president to drop over.

The vice-president was a man with a crew cut and blunt, concise opinions.

Sounds great, he said.

It's a winner, he said.

Bring the guy in, he said.

He was the first person to say something constructive. The Minister realized that they had to go to the forest to bring the guy in. They had to do it right away before the wolves, the bears, the elk, the mosquitoes, the plague, starvation, exposure, influenza killed him—or, God help us, the man deserted.

There wasn't a moment to lose.

He ordered the journalist to be taken into custody so that he wouldn't interfere with the operation. He was arrested for blatant misuse of a dead war hero's name and for offending the honor of the Finnish soldier.

Then he contacted the Border Patrol and told them to

get Käppärä from Tuokojärvi in Sevettilä parish. He assigned the sheriff of the county to show them the way: they were to take the man alive and uninjured, and he was to be handled with the greatest respect.

The general of the Border Patrol asked if Käppärä was a business magnate who'd been lost in a hunt. The Minister said that Käppärä was a soldier and hero and should be treated accordingly.

The general couldn't recall in what special ways heroic soldiers were treated; usually one buried them. But in peacetime, said the general, one made a fuss over ordinary people: this did not bode well for future wars.

The Minister said that he wasn't in the mood for such nonsense—the general should save it for the next government defense course. And so the general sent one of his helicopters to bring in Viktor Käppärä.

**The first thing** he heard was the sound.

It was an unfamiliar sound, and consequently many times more dangerous than the usual ones. Viktor grabbed his automatic pistol. The noise resembled the clatter of a broken machine gun, but it came from above. You had to be *really* on your guard when danger came from above; that much Viktor knew.

Then he saw the helicopter; it was flying right above the treetops. He'd never seen a helicopter before. And he'd never seen the rings on the body of the aircraft; they'd become the national symbol. More and more nations seemed to be involved: he'd seen an American, and for all he knew this plane could be from Australia. The Russians must be hurting if they had to keep sending their allies into combat all the time.

He bitterly regretted that he'd let the American sergeant go. Now they were really after him! Who else but that Yankee could have led them there?

Viktor fired a volley at the aircraft, which hovered in place in the air like a bee near a flower. The bullets split the rotor blades and the splinters flew all over and the helicopter dipped and plunged sharply into the lake.

Viktor jumped up and down and shouted Hurrah!, then danced a joyful victory dance. He'd shot down an Enemy aircraft!

It felt just terrific, not at all repugnant like shooting the

infiltrators. To kill people one can't see isn't unpleasant. It's like eating eggs; one doesn't have to kill the hen. Not that Viktor minded killing what he could eat; it was just senseless killing that he didn't care for. Viktor hated cats because they liked to kill, and the bloodthirstiness of wolverines horrified him. And yet all these were meek compared with humans who killed other humans recklessly and without cause.

Of course there were important provisions in the downed helicopter that Viktor badly needed, but he stopped himself from going after them. The aircraft was barely half-submerged and it would have been no great problem to get in, but he didn't want to see the crew. During his solitary years he'd grown very shy of people.

But Viktor's victory wasn't a purely happy one; victories in war seldom are. Out of the downed aircraft poured oil, polluting the waters of the little lake. The fish died and the sea birds got covered with grease and died a pitiful death. Viktor's chances of survival worsened considerably. He even began to consider a retreat, but he couldn't decide in which direction to retreat, and before he had time to decide he found himself under attack again.

**In addition to the pilot** in the downed helicopter there'd been an army officer, a doctor, a representative of the Ministry of the Interior, and the sheriff of Sevettilä. All of them died—one from head injuries, the others from drowning. The biographers absolve Viktor of any blame. Quite reasonably, they maintain that there was no way for him to have known that the air force had exchanged its swastika for white and blue rings. In this connection they call attention to the harm that can come of straying from tradition; it always causes unhappiness. According to the biographers, there was no reason to mistake the Finnish swastika for the German one. The Finnish swastika rested firmly on one of its long sides while the German one teetered precariously on one end, a prediction of things to come.

A discussion ensued among the biographers as to how the five deaths should be classified. Of course they'd occurred in peacetime, but the men had been killed in action and thus fulfilled the requirement for being "war heroes." But they'd been killed in action by the Finnish army, which did complicate the issue: if they were declared war heroes, there might emerge a deluge of liquidated Red Guards[43] or draft-dodgers demanding reconsideration of their status. Thus the incident was entered in the books as an accident in the same category as when a recruit is hazed to death or blown to bits in an accidental grenade explosion, or when a troop transport loaded with soldiers overturns in a ditch and kills them because the driver's had to drive thirty-six hours straight during a maneuver.

On the other hand, the biographers used several pages to praise Käppärä's courage and energy, which hadn't flagged with age. Furthermore, they couldn't see the slightest sign of defeatist tendencies; according to them, the battle demonstrated the perseverance of the Finnish soldier, whose morale in wartime overcomes all conceivable hardships.

These assertions were based on a number of distracted notes in Viktor's posthumous papers. At one point he says: "Mama, my pen's getting fainter and fainter; I can't see what I'm writing anymore."

On another piece of paper he scribbled: "Why is it so hard to breathe when I start walking fast? I don't think I'll be able to march home from here; they'll have to come and get me with horse and wagon."

Later: "It stings when I piss."

And: "I don't dream about women anymore; it's wonderful."

With his deteriorating vision Viktor's notes get shorter and harder to decipher. They become little cries of solitary desperation not directed at any living being; clearly it's not the end of the war but his own end that occupies his thoughts. But this the biographers do not concede; they say that he was alive and fighting single-handedly for victory. This is why, they say, it was a blessing that the man who sacrificed more for victory than any other soldier never learned that it was all in vain. For in war as in sports, there is something greater than victory—to play the game and never admit defeat even if one is seven laps behind. If there's such a thing as an offensive victory, there must also be a defensive one, and who has conferred more honor and glory on its name than Viktor Käppärä?

**Operation Käppärä** was a complete fiasco. The Minister of the Interior blamed the incompetence of the Border Patrol, and the military blamed the Minister of the Interior, who'd given misleading or insufficient information about the nature of the undertaking (which inevitably happens when civilians mix into military affairs). If they'd known that it was a question of approaching a military installation they would never have gone in the way they had; that was obvious. On the contrary, they'd had the impression that the operation was more like arranging the evacuation of an injured party.

The incident precipitated a cabinet crisis. The Foreign Minister—who wasn't from the same party as the Minister of the Interior—felt slighted because he hadn't been informed that the country's armed forces were still at war with the Soviet Union. The Defense Minister—who belonged to a third party—was also indignant; he felt that Käppärä fell directly under *his* jurisdiction. The Minister of Health and Welfare—who belonged to a fourth party— felt that he should have been personally informed if anyone in Finland didn't have housing or employment or health insurance and all the other services and rights—for example, the right to be alive after having been declared dead.

Cabinet crises, of course, occurred daily, and this one wasn't any more noteworthy than any other. The President dissolved the government and appointed another cabinet, in which the same ministers had different positions. All this while Viktor Käppärä sat in his dugout protecting the Fatherland. (The latter is no empty phrase, for as Käppärä's biographers point out many times in their book, no sacrifice has ever been in vain, no effort wasted, no vigilance unfounded, no attack unjustified, no defense measure meaningless, no danger merely imagined—and no solution better than a military one, the tried and true solution. And one never knows what would have happened if Käppärä *hadn't* stayed at his post.)

But now they wanted him out of there! This much the ministers in the new government (in which the former Minister of the Interior was the Minister of Health, the Foreign Minister was the Minister of the Interior, and the Minister of Defense the Minister of Agriculture, etc.) agreed on. So the order was given to the chief of the armed forces—while the Commander-in-Chief (the President) sat wondering how he was going to explain all this to the boys in the Kremlin.

The head of the Joint Chiefs of Staff gave the assignment to a captain by the name of Matalamäki. He was to retrieve the casualties from the helicopter and the survivor from his post, and each was to be delivered in the condition in which he was found, i.e., the dead dead and the living living, not vice versa. The order was clear and concise; there was no room for interpretation.

A reconnaissance plane had taken photographs of the crash, but they hadn't been able to investigate it because it was within Käppärä's firing range, and they didn't want to sacrifice more lives by exposing the crew of a rescue party to Enemy fire. (One was forced to speak at this point of "Enemy fire" because "friendly fire" had too paradoxical a ring to it and "comradely fire" had too many Marxist overtones.) Accordingly, the captain of the expedition should first neutralize (they'd have preferred a better word than "neutralize," but couldn't find one) Käppärä, and only thereafter devote his attention to the casualties.

The various phases of this operation have been recorded in detail, but for the less military-minded reader, the oral exchanges between Viktor and Captain Matalamäki will perhaps prove to be of no small interest.

The squad approached (stupidly!) Viktor's position from the northeast, where the Enemy would have come from had there been any. (To this day, Finland's armed forces are prepared to defend the country from any attack, regardless of the direction from which it comes: northeast, east, or southeast.) Viktor spotted the men, who made no attempt to camouflage their advance; they wanted him to see that his own troops were approaching. Viktor saw them (not as well as he might have twenty years before), took aim, and waited until they got so close that he couldn't miss; he couldn't afford to waste ammunition needlessly when Enemy activity kept increasing. The soldiers' gear confused him. He couldn't figure out which country they were from, but their uniforms and helmets reminded him most of the Americans. Obviously they'd been led there by the son of a bitch whom Viktor had stupidly decided not to shoot.

Once again Sergeant Hurmalainen had been right when he'd warned Viktor about infiltrators who pretended to be Finns. Viktor had seen a plane the last few days circling over the area and, sure enough, the leader of the squad started calling to him in Finnish.

Hello, he shouted, this is Captain Matalamäki speaking. I order you to throw down your weapons and march over here.

That's the way they always talked; always the same old line!

In reply, Viktor let loose a short burst of shots. There was no point hoping to surprise them when they already knew where he was.

That woke them up; the men dove for cover.

Are you crazy, shooting at your own men? shouted Captain Matalamäki.

My own men don't usually hide in the bushes and tell me to throw down my weapons, shouted Viktor back. Why don't you come and get my guns? Anyway, *you* might as well give up. You're surrounded by the Yellow Brigade. Better just drop your weapons and come out with your hands above your heads. It's your only chance.

Viktor thought it was worth trying a bluff: if they'd parachuted out of a plane, they might not know the area too well.

My good man! shouted the captain, who was beginning to get impatient. We're not at war anymore, so you can stop shooting.

If we're not at war, *you* throw down *your* weapons and give up, said Viktor.

The captain couldn't deny Viktor's logic, but he'd never heard or read in any handbook of a squad laying down its weapons except when they surrendered to the Enemy. And Käppärä, of course, wasn't an Enemy and, moreover, it was impossible to surrender in peacetime. The unexpected had happened—and now the brilliant clarity of the order was suddenly obscured. It wasn't going to work simply to go and get Private Käppärä and bring him back to the General Staff in the state in which he was found. It wasn't going to work at all. The captain wondered if there was something wrong with the order or with him. But he realized at once that it wasn't wise to countermand an order, the origin of all things: "In the beginning was the Order . . ."

He decided to try to stick to the letter of the law.

Dammit, soldier, shouted the captain, can't you obey orders?

That's exactly what I'm doing, Viktor answered.

But I'm giving you a *new* order! screamed the captain.

I don't take orders from anyone but the Supreme Field Marshal of Finland and Sergeant Hurmalainen, said Viktor.

Mannerheim is dead, said the captain.

Was he killed in action? said Viktor.

No, he died thirty years ago in Switzerland.[44] He was President, said Captain Matalamäki.

Aha, said Viktor, now *that* makes sense: we should have taken on Switzerland right away instead of fighting Russia. Russia's so big it'll take forever to Finlandize it.[45]

The captain thought Käppärä was putting him on: he couldn't imagine that the same term had originated both in Bonn and the woods of Sevettilä. But it wasn't his job to talk politics with a man who was still guarding a foxhole from the 1940s. The captain realized that the events of the last thirty years seemed unbelievable even to the people who'd experienced them; to tell them to Käppärä would be to present him with a future so incredible and impossible that he'd *never* leave his foxhole.

The captain made a last desperate attempt.

If you don't follow orders immediately, I'll suspend

your leaves till the end of the war! he screamed, and he'd scarcely said it before he wanted to bite his tongue.

Viktor responded with a burst of shots.

Then the sooner I end the war, the better! he shouted. The war can't end unless you fight!

The platoon lay low until it started to get dark. When the twilight mists swept in from the lake, Captain Matalamäki pulled his troops back, their mission still to be accomplished.

**The next day** the headline in the paper read: SOLITARY SENTRY ROUTS ENTIRE PLATOON, and all the press wondered out loud whether the armed forces of Finland were worth the cost of their uniforms. One columnist even suggested straight out that they should all be scrapped because they were rusted through and through, and therefore dangerous to national security. He asserted that talk of a military "vacuum" was just hokum; the only dangerous vacuum was the one in the generals' heads.

Of course no one took him seriously; militarism was so entrenched in the Finnish soul that even the Communists asked God in their evening prayers for a strong military that *they* would control. But the Leftist papers made sure to denigrate the Rightist-controlled army, and the Right registered horror and amazement at the armed forces' ineptitude; if lives could be lost that way, property was threatened too.

The Chief of Staff and all the generals of the General Staff were enraged that the rules of secrecy were no longer in effect. Gone were the good old days when, instead of cannons, the armed forces could place placards on all the islands in the Gulf of Finland reading "Off Limits" and they would be respected; gone were the days when they could put "Top Secret" on all requisition forms for everything from wartime cognac to toilet paper and these would be respected, too. Those were wonderful days when nobody knew anything and the military enjoyed universal respect.

It was all the press's fault; they stuck their noses into everything. The fact that the editors-in-chief had been brainwashed by government defense courses made no difference; they couldn't control their own staffs and so the editors disseminated, under the guise of news, Enemy propaganda against the armed forces.

Thanks to the press, the Americans had lost the Vietnam War. All the papers talked about were the setbacks, and they finally succeeded in convincing even the commanders of the fighting forces that they'd lost, even though there wasn't much left to destroy in Vietnam. It was the media that had knocked Nixon off his perch and turned his closest associates into scoundrels. Even his personal adviser, General Haig, was transferred to Europe, where he was made commander of NATO. There he was accused of using an official car to transport his dog from Bonn to Hamburg—as if one could expect that an American dog would know his way around Germany all by itself.

In general, people had turned against the military, and yet they were needed now more than ever. Who else could make use of all the weapons that had been produced since World War II at a cost of 60 billion dollars? Who else but the military could teach the illiterate people of the Third World to use their weapons, thereby creating a need for more of them? The annual cost of weapons already exceeded the national income of all the Third World nations combined. In spite of the advances in technology, the human factor was still the deciding one. Industry could never survive without the help of the military; that is why it was so repugnant for them to see how the capitalist-controlled press yapped at them. Yet in spite of the camouflage they wore on maneuvers, the military couldn't see through democracy's camouflage.

Obviously, the generals had the means at their disposal to eliminate, annihilate, destroy, wipe out, drug, poison, gas, and pacify Private Käppärä, but not without risking injury to him. Also, after several days of deliberation, they realized what an asset Käppärä could be for the defense spirit; they'd be able to compare him to both Poet Laureate Runeberg and Field Marshal Mannerheim. No, the usual methods wouldn't do at all.

While the high command raged on about freedom of the press, someone remembered that the journalist who had written about Käppärä, thereby bringing him to national attention, was still in jail. He was *de facto* the only person who had seen Käppärä and spoken with him without losing his life. If he'd done it once, he could do it again. A decision was made to send the journalist to negotiate with Käppärä. If he succeeded in persuading Viktor to return to civilization, they would drop the indictment against him.

The journalist accepted. This time, he said to himself, he had the chance of a lifetime to get the scoop every true journalist dreams of!

A committee was appointed to think of arguments that might conceivably get Käppärä to give up his stiff-necked resistance. But they made the same mistake that the editors of weekly magazines and heads of advertising agencies are guilty of: they assumed that Viktor was a "simple man" with the approximate intellectual capacity of a twelve-year-old. (His biographers, of course, described him as a Superman.)

When one brilliant fellow figured out that Viktor was still living in the forties, the committee tried to decide what a half-retarded private in those times would want most. They came up with the following: the journalist should promise Käppärä that as soon as he returned home he'd go to Berlin and shake Adolph Hitler's hand. He'd also get a personal citation from Field Marshal Mannerheim and twice the ration cards he was entitled to. He'd get a fishing boat with an outboard motor and free fuel for the rest of his life. He'd dance with Miss Finland at the Independence Ball in the Presidential Palace.

When the journalist pointed out that not all of these promises could be kept, the chairman of the committee agreed, saying, however, that all of them could be replaced with even better ones, ones that the soldier might at this point find incomprehensible: he couldn't be expected to know about television sets, mopeds, blow-up life-size party dolls, and group charters to Majorca.

Much of the discussion centered on what the journalist should wear on the expedition. He rejected all suggestions from a general's uniform to a coat and tails with the sensible observation that the best thing would be for him to dress as he had the first time, or Käppärä wouldn't recognize him.

Finally the journalist was flown to Sevettilä and carried by jeep to the other side of Tuokojärvi, from where he had just a short walk to the outpost. What happened there has never been fully known; after about half an hour, however, the troop heard a shot, and they never saw the journalist again.

"What I need are glasses, aspirin, and a mailbox to put my letters in," Viktor commented in an undated note that might conceivably be interpreted as a comment on the offer he'd received from the committee. That he didn't trust the journalist, however, was obvious; even the General Staff got the idea.

But the journalist's death didn't put an end to the news items in the papers. On the contrary, it became front-page material across the globe. The eyes of the world were suddenly focused on a man who, unaware of all the excitement, was sitting and polishing his rifle in a hole in the forest while a journalist lay in another hole doing nothing at all.

**Captain Matalamäki** was the only person left who'd had direct contact with Käppärä. When the outlines of a new strategy were being drawn up, he was called in for consultation. But he didn't have much to contribute; according to him, there was *no* way to take Käppärä alive.

If all soldiers were like Viktor Käppärä, wars would never end if the commanders-in-chief happened to die before they had time to call off the hostilities. Loyalty like his gladdened the heart of the commander of the armed forces, who felt that the periods of peace between wars had a lamentably deleterious effect on the troops. He felt a strong commitment to the youth of Finland, whom he wished to protect both physically and psychologically: this could be done most effectively in the battlefields where danger lurked. Young people should be kept away from drugs and alcohol and motorcycles and loose women (the liberated ones were the worst). Also, he supported the modern concept of annihilating the civilian population and preserving the military one, which, after the cessation of hostilities, could be used in the service of the victorious side. In the past, wars had tried to inflict only superficial damage on the military-industrial complex; for even though a Krupp and a Morgan might be on opposing sides, they were working for the same cause: profits that were influenced by neither victory nor defeat. But the lessons of World War II showed that the best ally was in the losers, and both the Americans and Russians could with confidence point to *their* German army that was ready to fight on their behalf. In other words, one had begun to protect the *whole* military establishment who didn't need to be retrained—unlike the often ideologically troublesome civilian population. Soldiers are and remain soldiers in whoever's pay they happen to find themselves; and as long as obedience is their watchword they need no other.

The best example of this thesis was Private Käppärä. He'd arrived like a godsend, an answer to a prayer to save all that was clean and sacred and beautiful. Now the young people would have a hero to look up to; again there'd be pride in donning a uniform. But this beautiful future threatened to collapse before it began if the stubborn idiot (this slipped out of the commander's mouth) didn't stop shooting at everyone who tried to talk sense to him. For a moment the general even considered dressing up the actor Joel Rinne[46] as Field Marshal Mannerheim and sending him to Sevettilä. But then he remembered that the moron of a captain had told him that Mannerheim had died (how could an Immortal be dead!). He pointed out to the captain the indiscretion of spreading rumors at the front that could worsen the morale of the combat forces.

The captain apologized, at the same time calling attention to the fact that he hadn't said that Sergeant Hurmalainen was dead.

Who the hell is Sergeant Hurmalainen? asked the general.

The captain said that he didn't know. Käppärä had said that aside from Mannerheim he took orders only from Sergeant Hurmalainen. Apparently Hurmalainen had been Käppärä's immediate superior.

The general ordered the captain to find the sergeant

immediately and send him to Sevittilä to demobilize Käppärä. By the following day the captain could report that he'd found Hurmalainen at his home in Vimpele but that he'd absolutely refused to have anything to do with the whole business.

The commander of the armed forces couldn't believe his ears; exasperated, he asked what the hell was going on. If Sergeant Hurmalainen wasn't dead, thundered the general, he had no right not to do his duty.

General, said Captain Matalamäki, the fact of the matter is that the sergeant isn't a sergeant anymore. Right after the armistice he was demoted to private, and he says that a buck private can't give orders to another one.

Crushed, the general sank into his chair. But he hadn't become general for lack of imagination: he said that since the demotion occurred after the armistice, Käppärä didn't know about it. Hurmalainen could *act* like a sergeant even if he wasn't one anymore.

The captain informed the general that the sergeant wouldn't go along with that kind of deception; he'd been Born Again.

Capital! exclaimed the general. He's a good Christian, and a good Christian is a good soldier. He's repented his sins, and among them no doubt is the offense that caused his demotion. We too can show our capacity for forgiveness and restore him to his former rank. So Hurmalainen is a sergeant again and I order him to release Private Viktor Käppärä immediately from all former duties. Understood?

A breath of the Divine wafted into the room. There is nothing so grand as the feeling of raising or lowering a human being with a mere word. The general discovered once again that there is even greater satisfaction in governing than in killing and destroying, and he felt a mild sting of regret that military coups weren't part of the Nordic pattern of behavior.

His regret soon increased considerably when the captain came back with the depressing news that the sergeant didn't want to be a sergeant and that he didn't give a hoot about "earthly matters." This was unfathomable—much worse than the general had dared to think. Clearly, civilian life had completely demoralized a perfectly good fellow. With surprise he looked at Hurmalainen's military record, which was sprinkled with the names of glorious battlefields, and he noted that this former noncom had been awarded three medals for valor. Then he lost his temper. What were all the VFW organizations for the preservation of church and society doing? Nothing! They too had been poisoned by the defeatist spirit of the times and had abandoned the country to its fate (Communism!).

Nothing like this would ever happen in the Soviet Union, said the general. (According to him, in the Soviet Union there was discipline, obedience, resourcefulness, defense spirit, willingness to sacrifice, and loving patriotism; sometimes it grieved him that, unlike officers of the Gustavian period, he couldn't serve under the Russians too.[47] There one surely would have learned to toe the line!) The captain cleared his throat and ventured the observation that the military did have its own head chaplain. The general looked at him, wondering if he would make good material for major, then said softly that he'd assign the chaplain the task of bringing Hurmalainen to his senses. As usual, in the darkest hour of need, Our Lord came to the rescue.

**What followed** is almost too distressing to relate. The chaplain expected to meet a brother in Christ, and he approached the former soldier with the same respect that Runeberg had shown Ensign Stål by the dusky waves of Näsijärvi.[48] And Hurmalainen wouldn't have had to sit around endlessly bragging about his military exploits; all that was required of him was one sentence, and he and the old Ensign would go down in history side by side. But what did the chaplain find? An arrogant apostate instead of a humble servant of the Lord!

The chaplain chose his words carefully.

I understand with all my heart, he said, that you do not feel you can make an end to a war that was originally God's will. But now it has come to pass that the Lord has changed His plan: He has let the weapons fall silent, and He wishes also that His lost son in the wilderness heed His voice, lay down his rifle, and return to the fold, which thanks him for the salvation of this country. As his instrument Our Lord has chosen you; praise the Lord that you are the Chosen One.

And Hurmalainen answered:

God knows what He's doing and He doesn't forget anyone, not even Viktor. It was *His* will that many souls stayed in the woods and swamps of the Karelian wilderness, and if He Himself hasn't told Viktor to leave, then He must want him to stay. It isn't up to me, a poor sinner, to change His purpose.

Our Lord has chosen to speak through you to His lost son, said the chaplain patiently.

I spoke with the Lord this morning, and He didn't say a word about it to me, said Hurmalainen.

In that case perhaps Our Lord wished to use the official channels of communication and sent me to deliver His message to you, said the chaplain, smiling.

That's just the way a lot of good messages get distorted, said Hurmalainen. All the chaplains I heard during the war told me to kill even though it says just the opposite in the Good Book.

The chaplain was used to laymen misinterpreting the Lord's true intention by taking Him at His word, so the criticism didn't offend him. Instead, he chose to try to trap Hurmalainen by asking him what God had said to him that morning.

God said the same thing He says every morning, said Hurmalainen. He says: Johannes, you're a drunk and you'll be one the rest of your life, so just don't drink today and naught ill shall befall you. That's what he's said to me for twenty years, and I've never had to take Antabuse.[49] But would the chaplain be kind enough to tell me what God said to *him* today?

I know my duties, and when I fulfill them I fulfill His will also, said the chaplain. Therefore, I have no need to trouble Him over trivialities. I know that His time is taken up with all the great troubles that fill the world.

I see! Is He *that* busy? said Hurmalainen. That makes me even more amazed and grateful that He takes time every morning to talk to me, a poor bricklayer.

Let us praise the Lord that in this free country we can turn to Him with our prayers! said the chaplain. What does the sergeant think would happen if the Communists came and robbed us of our freedom?

To tell you the truth, said Hurmalainen, I think they'll

come if they want to come and if you really intend to use Viktor to stop them from coming, the best thing would be to leave him at his post.

So you propose to let the poor man die and molder away in the wilderness? said the chaplain.

He wouldn't be the only one. Thousands of his comrades-in-arms are out there to keep him company. At least they're not war-crazy like the ones he'd meet at home who apparently want to use him like the Pied Piper of Hamlin to lure new children into the depravity of war!

The chaplain had infinite pity for this unbending man who couldn't see that the Devil had merely changed shape when he traded the bottle for the Book. Literature is meant for a small elite, not for people who let themselves be led astray by the messages in books.

Deeply saddened, his mission still unaccomplished, the chaplain left the bricklayer's home, suddenly understanding why Jesus never laughed: everything was so terribly distressing.

**When a man grows larger** than his destiny, Death's scythe inevitably cuts him down to size. Such was the case with John Kennedy, Mahatma Gandhi, Abraham Lincoln, and Martin Luther King, to name just a few.

Nothing could save Viktor Käppärä, either.

He'd started out as a small worry for the Finns, but now he had grown into a worldwide symbol of resistance. In the West he'd become the sentry against Communism and the Asian horde, and in the East he represented the proletarians' indomitability in the struggle for the Fatherland (Workers of the world, unite!); in Africa the new nationalism embraced him as its hero, and in South America he was compared to Che Guevara (who had also grown larger than his destiny), and every munitions factory across the world began to spit out Viktor Käppärä products. Finland had lost exclusive rights to its hero. In fact, he'd become impossible to tolerate as a reality; he had to be kept in the shadow world, the source of mankind's tragedies whose greatness can be measured only by their inexplicability.

There weren't many choices left. Finland could only try to make the publicity around Viktor as profitable as possible. They planned one last rescue attempt (rescue from what?) which would be televised and broadcast worldwide via satellite, like the Olympic Games. They figured on making ten times as much money as world

heavyweight champion Muhammed Ali had ever earned for a match.

In fact, like Ali, Viktor Käppärä was billed as the greatest, the strongest, and the prettiest. However, the drawings of him (of course there weren't any photographs) resembled Jesus—Jesus always looks the same no matter who draws Him—in order to emphasize his suffering, the suffering soldier who suffered for humanity. Viktor's biographers (who were certified patriots) regretted that these Jesus pictures had so few typically Finnish features. Fortunately, Jesus had very few Jewish features, too, which made it possible for Albert Edelfelt to put him in his painting in a grove of Finnish birches by a lake that could have been Tuokojärvi.[50]

Viktor appeared in many forms: Jesus discharging a new Bofors gun; Jesus with a Krupp machine gun; Jesus with a Czechoslovakian bazooka; Jesus as a pilot in the latest-model MIG. This time, Jesus had returned properly armed; there was no longer any risk that He'd allow Himself to be crucified. It was clear that now it was mankind's turn.

But Viktor didn't know anything about all this. He didn't know that long-range TV lenses were trained on his outpost; and he didn't know that a whole company was crawling toward the Finnish army's last defensive position in World War II; and he didn't know that approximately 100 million pairs of eyes were waiting for the battle that was soon to begin. Viktor also didn't know what the viewers knew—that the Enemy (the army of the Republic of Finland) was shooting at him with blanks. The intention was to give the illusion of a normal attack and force the sentry to return their fire until he'd used up all his ammunition. They figured that it would be over quickly; no matter how sparing Käppärä had been, he couldn't have many bullets left after thirty years. And when he'd shot his last shot they figured that he would let himself be taken prisoner (they had no other adequate term for it), and the whole world would behold the hero (the Finn) who'd never surrendered. (The TV directors were concerned that they couldn't make Viktor up. The audience had been spoiled by TV heroes always looking as neat at the end of a show as they'd been at the beginning, no matter what they'd had to go through.)

As far as Viktor was concerned, it wasn't a good day for a battle. He had stomach pains and heartburn, as well as a headache and difficulty pissing. He often got cramps in the fingers of his right hand, and, if something upset him, his heart started to palpitate. Recently he'd got upset a lot; to kill people didn't suit him at all. He couldn't sleep, and he'd begun to imagine that the dead men had started to move again and were just waiting for a chance to kill him in revenge for what he'd done to them.

He'd begun to talk to them, trying to explain his situation, asking what else he could have done. He'd had to kill; he'd been ordered to do it. He said that they should go after the ones who were really responsible—somebody had to be responsible. It disturbed him that he couldn't furnish their names and addresses. (And here he touched on the hollow solution to the Great Enigma. No war starts before those responsible have convinced the population that it's *their* will, that they themselves are the cause of their own unhappiness.)

When the firing began, Viktor slipped into his foxhole and prepared to fight off his attackers. He still had two clips left for his automatic pistol and about a hundred rounds for his rifle, half a dozen hand grenades, and the flare gun he'd intended to shoot off at the victory celebration. All those years he'd worried that the rocket wouldn't ignite; he'd wanted to make the end of the war as festive as possible.

The Enemy fire was heavy, but it was too high: he couldn't hear the bullets whistling. Of course it might have been because his hearing had gotten worse; for some time he hadn't heard the crickets chirping either. And he couldn't see the Enemy; this time they'd taken proper cover. But he thought he saw bushes swaying, and he fired some shots, hoping to keep them at a distance. To be prepared for fighting at close quarters he took the safety off the hand grenades he'd placed in front of him like eggs in a bird's nest. The one thing that gave him hope was that the Enemy wasn't using heavier weapons; they didn't even have trench mortars with them.

Afraid that his attackers would think that he was killed and then come even closer, he answered their fire: he hoped that the Enemy would give up before his ammunition ran out.

They didn't.

Viktor understood that he couldn't expect any mercy when even the dead were against him, and he realized that if he wanted to find out if the rocket would work, he had to fire it now. What happened subsequently will remain as much of a mystery as the murder of President Kennedy. The people who sat before their TV sets saw a star suddenly ignite against the night sky, and for a moment it stood still above the birch tree that grew next to Viktor's camp, then sailed toward the lake and went out.

A muffled explosion followed, and when the attacking troop finally ventured toward the dugout, all they found was a hole, nothing else. There was nothing left of the sentry; it was as if he'd never been there.

In fact, that was what most of the TV viewers ended up believing. When they didn't see the corpse they felt they'd been duped; it had all been a hoax. The least one could expect for paying tax on a color TV set (which every owner did) was to see blood, but instead all they saw was a hole the neighbor's dog might have dug in one's garden.

# Notes

1. Johan Ludvig Runeberg (1804–77) is Finland's "national poet"; his works—all written in Swedish—have become the property, in Finnish translation, of the entire nation. The poem alluded to here is Number 25 in the first collection of "Idyll och epigram" ("Idylls and Epigrams") in Runeberg's *Dikter: Andra häftet* (*Poems: Second Collection*, 1833). Beset by failing harvests, the heroically patient Paavo has his wife mix bark into their bread—first "a half portion" and then a double portion; at last, fortune smiles on Paavo, but he still gives the same instruction to his wife: "Mix thou in the bread a half of bark still,/ For all frost-nipped stand our neighbour's fields" (*Johan Ludvig Runeberg's Lyrical Songs, Idylls and Epigrams*, done into English by Eirikr Magnusson and E. H. Palmer [London: John Bentley, 1878], p. 205).

"Iki-Kianto" was the sobriquet of the novelist Ilmari Kianto (1874–1970), the author of two classic novels about backwoods life in east-central Finland, *Punainen viiva* (*The Red Line*, 1909), and *Ryysyrannan Jooseppi* (*Joseph of Ryysyranta*, 1924). It has been noted by the essayist Johannes Salminen that, in contrast to Runeberg's idealization, "Finnish poverty has been stripped of all of its redeeming features in Ilmari Kianto; a northern hunger-land appears which breaks people down instead of stoically hardening them" (in the essay "Images of the People" in Salminen's *Gränsland* [Helsinki: Söderström & Co., 1984], p. 70).

2. Kianto's "castle in the wilderness" was his home, Turjanlinna (literally, "Troll's Castle"), in eastern Suomussalmi parish. In fact, the episode described took place in the aftermath of the

Winter War (1939–40); Kianto was sentenced to six months' imprisonment by the Finnish authorities. Tikkanen remembered the aged Kianto (*Mariegatan 26 Kronohagen*, [Helsinki: Söderström & Co., 1977], p. 69): "an author who had been stuck into prison during the war because he wrote a message on the back of a cigarette box, asking the enemy not to burn his house which lay in the zone of combat. In his books he had fought passionately for the poorest and most indigent members of society, people had forgiven him that, but that he had also asked the Bolsheviks to spare his house—that was unpardonable."

3. The Swedish-Russian War of 1808–1809, during which Finland passed from the Swedish crown to the czar, provided the material for Runeberg's double suite of patriotic poems, *Fänriks Ståls sägner* (*The Tales of Ensign Stål*, 1848–60).

Jakov Petrovitch Kulnev (1764–1812), a Russian field commander in that war, enjoyed great popularity in Finland because of his reputed good nature and gallantry; he is celebrated by Runeberg—who, as a four-year-old, is supposed to have been dandled at the Russian's knee, when Kulnev's cossacks occupied Jakobstad, the poet's birthplace, in March, 1808—in the canto "Kulneff" of *Fänrik Stål*. Tikkanen (who no doubt had had to memorize *Fänrik Stål* in school) refers to stanza three of the long eulogy: "And girls—how well he knew the way/ To fetch the fair ones at his call!/ He'd scarce have left a bloody fray/ But he would give a ball;/ And when the furious night was through,/ He'd take his little favorite's shoe/ And fill it from the nearest bowl/ To quaff a parting skoal" (*The Tales of Ensign Stål*, tr. by Charles Wharton Stork [New York: American-Scandinavian Foundation, 1960], p. 68).

4. Carl Gustaf Mannerheim (1867–1951) served as an officer in the Chevalier Guard at St. Petersburg in the early 1890s; he was particularly popular at the court because of his knowledge of riding and his elegant manner. (He was one of the young officers

designated to bear the baldachin sheltering Nicholas II at the latter's coronation.)

5. Risto Ryti (1889–1956) had become president in December, 1940. The literary scholar Yrjö Hirn is supposed to have said to Tikkanen's paternal grandmother that the war was bound to go wrong with a spiritualist as president and a sports enthusiast as prime minister. The latter reference is to Johan Wilhelm Rangell (1894–1982).

6. After the victory of the White forces in Finland's Civil War (January–May, 1918), summary executions of the Red prisoners were common, both outside and inside the camps. As a child, living with his maternal grandparents in Lahti, Tikkanen had heard stories of "the many Reds who were shot in the prison camp at Lahti during the Civil War. But the stories were told to me in a way that caused me not to feel sorry for [the victims] at all" (*Brändövägen 8. Brändö Tel 35* [Helsinki: Söderström & Co., 1976], p. 33). Hennala, where Hurmalainen's father was killed, is a cantonment in Lahti.

7. The capital of Eastern Karelia, Petroskoi (Russian: Petrozavodsk), on the western side of Lake Onega, was captured by the Finnish army on October 1, 1941, and renamed Äänislinna. Karhumäki (Russian: Medvesya Gora), at the lake's northern tip, was taken on December 5. The Finns had already set up a defensive line along the Syväri (Russian: Svir) River, which connects Lakes Onega and Ladoga, and then advanced beyond it. In his diary from the Continuation War, the essayist and journalist Olavi Paavolainen (1903–61) describes the almost mystical importance of the Syväri—"the legendary 'holy' river of the AKS"—for those Finns who believed in the expansion of Finland to the east and the inclusion of the East Karelians in a Greater Finland. (See Olavi Paavolainen, *Synkkä yksinpuhelu: Päiväkirjan lehtiä vuosilta 1941–44* [Helsinki: Otava, 1982], p. 140, entry for September 29, 1941.) The Akateeminen Karjala-Seura, a student organization founded by former participants in the abortive (and illegal) Finnish expeditions to East Karelia in

the wake of the Civil War, had a "racist" and expansionist program that eventually provided an ideological pretext for Finland's co-belligerency with Germany in the Continuation War.

8. Joseph Goebbels (1897–1945) was Adolf Hitler's minister of propaganda.

9. In Eastern Europe, the German army had been engaged in a slow withdrawal—customarily described in remarkable circumlocutions—since the defeat at Stalingrad in February, 1943. Paavolainen notes one of these (*Synkkä yksinpuhelu*, p. 324, February 16, 1943): "One of the most fantastic new terms is used for the front between Charkhov and Kursk, 'fluent defensive action with wandering islands of resistance.'"

10. Hitler flew to Finland on June 4, 1942, to participate—quite unexpectedly—in the celebration of Mannerheim's birthday; on June 28, Mannerheim visited the Führer in turn. In his entry for July 8, Paavolainen described the newsreel footage: "The marshal is quite wonderful with his walking stick, his earnest expression, and his handkerchief, which he touches to his lips time and time again—an incomparable gesture of discreet scorn. A representative of the *ancien régime*, aristocratically self-assured and refined, at whose side Hitler, laughing in his vulgar way, appears an upstart pure and simple, a genuine housepainter's assistant, as he slaps the marshal on the shoulder" (*Synkkä yksinpuhelu*, p. 222).

11. Ernst von Born (1885–1956)—who in fact had been minister of the interior in 1931–32 and 1939–41, but who was later minister of justice in Mannerheim's cabinet—was Tikkanen's special bête noire, appearing as "Vilhelm von Rudas" in *Hjältarna är döda* and then, unmasked, in *Brändövägen 8*: he had evidently been the first of several lovers of Tikkanen's mother. Early on in *Brändövägen 8* (p. 22), Tikkanen tells how von Born begged

her to run away with him, how the child they had conceived together was aborted, and about von Born's arrogance and lack of physical attraction—"I don't believe for a moment that mother really loved the child's father." During the Continuation War, his mother married "a common soldier" (the sculptor Sakari Tohka), and "then the minister deserted her, was there anything more worthless than a soldier? . . . The marriage had also released the minister who had loved her so much from his responsibility. He had transformed that love which had brought her misfortune to the nation itself, and it looked as if the story were going to be repeated." (The passage in the printed texts mentions only an unspecified "minister" and says nothing about his voice. The present details were added by Tikkanen in a conversation with the translator. In his diary for September 2, 1944 (*Synkkä yksinpuhelu*, p. 562), Olavi Paavolainen described the radio speech of Prime Minister Anders Hackzell about peace terms, and noted Hackzell's "hoarse and tired voice." Can Tikkanen, in his detestation of von Born, have misremembered?)

12. See *Brändövägen 8* (pp. 18–19): "My mother's first prominent lover was an aristocratic politician from the Swedish People's Party. He was so infinitely rich that he regarded himself as a liberal and insisted that [after the Civil War] no tenant farmers had been shot on his estate." (Ernst von Born owned Sarvlax Estate in eastern Uusimaa.) In *Bävervägen 11 Hertonäs* (Helsinki: Söderström & Co., 1976), pp. 140–41, Tikkanen told the story of the seduction again. One summer at Sarvlax, his father, plied with alcohol, had fallen asleep, and "[von Born] enchanted Mother with the many cylinders in his large black Stutz and the many beautiful oaks in the park, which was also his."

13. The place names in the novel are fictional; it is to be assumed that the action takes place somewhere near the eastern (Soviet) border of the province of Pohjois-Karjala (North Karelia).

14. The episode, from the War of 1808–1809, is described in the canto "Sandels," of *Fänrik Stål*. The commander of the Swedish-Finnish forces, Johan August Sandels, refused to interrupt his

meal, despite the news that the Russians—following Russian time, not Swedish—had ended an armistice an hour early; he then rode to the battlefield and saved the day.

15. Paavo Nurmi (1897–1973) achieved world fame by his victories at the Olympic Games of 1920 and 1924 (in the latter of which Tikkanen's father had also taken part, as a member of the marksmanship team). Nurmi's American tour of 1925 got him the nickname "the Flying Finn," on the analogy of "the Flying Scot," Eric Lidell, another great track star of the 1924 games.

16. Swedish: *polityrgubbe* or *puligubbe;* Finnish: *puliukko* or, simply, *puli,* terms for homeless derelicts, reputed to be willing to drink anything with an alcoholic content, even furniture polish. Tikkanen describes them (and his acquaintances among them) several times in his autobiographical work.

17. Hietaniemi (Sandudd) Cemetery in Helsinki; in *Georgsgatan* (Helsinki: Söderström & Co., 1980), pp. 56–57, Tikkanen has a long description of "this cemetery, [where] meglomania flourished unconcealed, which was one side of this people with [their] low self-esteem." He also notes that Aleksis Kivi, "Finnish literature's greatest genius," was confined at Lapinlahti Asylum, which lies in the middle of the great cemetery; in *Brändövägen 8,* he observes that his own great-grandfather, Paavo Tikkanen, ended his days there. In the sequel to *30-åriga kriget, Efter hjältedöden* (Helsinki: Söderström & Co., 1979), p. 125, Viktor Käppärä is likewise locked up in the asylum: "he got the same room as two other mythomaniacs, Aleksis Kivi and Mika Waltari [the twentieth-century novelist], had in their days."

18. Vimpele (Swedish: Vindala) is in Ostrobothnia. In *Efter hjältedöden,* however, Hurmalainen's wife's name is Jenny and they live somewhere near Nastola in southern Finland. Viktor, who is not dead after all, finds Hurmalainen there, and enjoys the company of "his old friend, who conversed with his God, but

reluctantly received His commands from Jenny" (p. 99), a militant feminist and very bossy.

19. Propagandists for a "Greater Finland" (on the analogy of Adolf Hitler's "Gross-Deutschland") dreamed of a nation that would include much of the northeastern Soviet Union and, of course, its Finno-Ugric peoples (see note 7 above).

20. *Tuntematon sotilas* (1955) of Väinö Linna (1920– ) has become the classic Finnish novel about the Continuation War (1941–44) and, despite its depiction of war's horrors, has often been employed as a patriotic and inspiratory text. In *Efter hjältedöden* (pp. 40–41), Viktor Käppärä—in his old uniform from 1944 and with his rifle on his shoulder—makes his way to Sevettilä (which has grown from a "church-village" to a "market town" to a "city"). The first person he meets is a little boy who asks him if he is "Rokka," the most famous of the soldiers depicted by Linna in *Tuntematon sotilas*—a witty and talkative Karelian who is also an expert and efficient killer of Russians. The boy has seen the film made from the novel on Finnish television, where it is frequently shown. In *Brändövägen 8* (p. 105), Tikkanen wrote: "Against their will, Mailer and Linna and [Joseph] Heller have created exalted heroic epics [*heroiserande hjälteepos*] on which war-enthusiasts unwittingly feast."

21. The "Atlantic Wall" was the name given by the German high command to the system of coastal fortifications in Brittany, Normandy, and along the Pas de Calais intended to repulse an Allied invasion. The landing, however, was successfully carried out on June 6, 1944.

22. Prohibition was introduced in Finland by the law of June 1, 1919, and from the outset did more harm than good, leading to widespread smuggling, illegal stills, and speakeasies. After a plebiscite, it was at last done away with on April 5, 1932. The parallels with Prohibition in the United States are obvious. Living in the skerries, Viktor's father, of course, was a smuggler.

23. Tikkanen refers to the long Baltic coastline of imperial Russia, from the river that divided Sweden and Finland in the north to the Courland Lagoon in the south, along the line separating Russian Lithuania from German East Prussia.

24. Tuokojärvi is the imaginary lake and district in "Sevettilä parish" where the novel's action takes place.

25. For Petroskoi and Karhumäki, see note 7 above; Poventsa (Russian: Povenets) lies east of the latter, at the southern terminus of the Stalin Canal, from Onega to the White Sea. This is the sector, by the way, where the young volunteer, Tikkanen, finally got to the front, after having asked his two half-brothers to arrange a transfer for him from the rear echelon (at Lappeenranta) where he had been stationed. One of the brothers was on the Karelian Isthmus, the other on the Murmansk railroad. "Finally the northerly brother succeeded and, happy in spirit, I went by way of Petroskoi to Karhumäki" (*Brändövägen 8*, pp. 102–3).

26. See note 7 above.

27. In the later 1940s, some Finns, fearing a coup by the Communists, deposited caches of firearms in the countryside. Tikkanen makes fun of the practice in his depiction of the atmosphere of postwar Helsinki in *Mitt Helsingfors* (Helsinki: Söderström & Co., 1972), pp. 51–52: "My old schoolmates buried weapons at their summer places, awaiting the next chance for revenge."

28. Väinö Tanner (1881–1966) was the leader of Finland's Social Democrats and, for a time, foreign minister in Ryti's cabinet.

29. Juho Kusti Paasikivi (1870–1956) was president of Finland from 1946 to 1956 and, as such, the creator of the so-called Paasikivi-Kekkonen line of peaceful and realistic cooperation with the Soviet Union.

30. After the Red Army had begun its devastating offensive on the Karelian Isthmus in June, 1944, President Ryti gave his personal pledge to the German foreign minister, Joachim von Ribbentrop, that Finland would not conclude a separate peace with the Soviet Union unless Germany agreed; in return, Finland was promised air cover and armaments.

31. In a "war guilt trial," Ryti, Tanner, and six other members of the wartime government were given prison terms, Ryti receiving the longest sentence, ten years. He was freed for reasons of health in 1949; Tanner, after his release, re-entered Finnish politics, not retiring until 1963.

32. When Ryti had resigned, on August 1, 1944, he was succeeded in the presidency by Mannerheim, who immediately declared that he was not obliged to honor the Ribbentrop Pact; peace negotiations with the Soviet Union were begun, and the Russians required that Finland sever its relations with Germany and disarm or expel the German troops in the country. The 20th Mountain Division, under Lothar Rendulic, resisted, and the so-called Lapland War ensued, during which the Germans, retreating through northern Finland toward Norway, followed a scorched-earth policy. The last fighting took place in April, 1945; losses had been heavy on both sides, all the more since the Finnish forces consisted mainly of young draftees. Looking back on this epilogue to the war, Tikkanen says that the immediate postwar days were puritanical in sexual matters, "while no one really accused the Germans in earnest for their burning of Lapland" (*Bävervägen 11 Hertonäs*, p. 27).

33. The nude bronze statue of Nurmi by Wäinö Aaltonen (1894–1966), from 1924–25, has stood at the Olympic Stadium in Helsinki since 1951. Nurmi is said to have been embarrassed by its intimate details.

34. Eino S. Repo (1919– ) was general director of Finland's radio system from 1965 to 1969; pressure from conservative circles caused his removal.

35. In 1971, a Swedish scholar, Thomas Henrikson, published *Romantik och Marxism: Estetik och politik hos Otto Ville Kuusinen och Diktonius* (*Romanticism and Marxism: Esthetics and Politics in Otto Ville Kuusinen and Diktonius*), a study of the exchanges, literary and personal, between Kuusinen (1881–1964), who was minister of education and the central ideologue in the Red government during Finland's civil war, and Elmer Diktonius (1896–1961), a young music student who — perhaps thanks to Kuusinen's influence—turned to revolutionary poetry. Later, Kuusinen, "the great survivor," became a right-hand man to Lenin, Stalin, and Khrushchev, and mentor to Andropov; Diktonius became a central figure in Scandinavian literary modernism.

36. Henri Désiré Landru (1869–1922), called "Bluebeard" by the French press, was guillotined on February 25, 1922, yet the text says that Käppärä was born on February 22. The psychiatrist also errs on a second point: Landru was scarcely driven to mass killings by "enforced abstinence." He enjoyed sexual relations with many of the 283 women who fell prey to his confidence schemes, and, as well, with some of his eleven murder victims.

37. Tikkanen elaborates on a passage in one of the best-known children's stories of Zacharias Topelius (1818–98), "Princessan Lindagull" in *Läsning för barn*, vol. 1 (1848). The princess has been kidnaped by the Lappish troll Hirmu. In an effort to force her to marry his son, Hirmu sends "a cloud of Lapland's hungry mosquitoes" to the cave where she is kept prisoner, "thousands and thousands upon thousands, until they filled the whole cave like thick smoke." She is saved by a tightly woven veil, carried to her by dreams from the looms of the fairies. "The mosquitoes could not penetrate this veil, they did not taste royal blood that day and that night."

Tikkanen quotes Runeberg's description of Suomenlinna (Sveaborg), the fortress-complex in Helsinki harbor: "Gibraltar's equal in our north" ("Sveaborg" in *Fänrik Stål*). The irony of the allusion lies in the fact that the Gibraltar of the North was surrendered to the Russians without a fight in May, 1808, by its commander, Karl Olof Cronstedt, an event described with utter scorn by Runeberg in his poem.

38. See note 34 above.

39. "But, after all, you have to have an enemy."

40. Urho Kekkonen (1900– ) was president from 1956 to October, 1981.

41. An explosion at the munitions factory in Lapua in Ostrobothnia, in 1976, caused the death of forty workers. In *Georgsgatan* (p. 76), Tikkanen has a further comment on the explosion. "[The president] was forced to think about the new gun-powder factory in Lapua. . . . The old one had already been so safe that, a day after it was blown to smithereens, a colonel said he would have gladly worked in it. But since only women worked in it, he no doubt meant that he'd have been glad to let his wife work there."

42. Kekkonen served in the White Army during the Civil War; during his regular (drafted) military service, in 1919–20, he rose to the rank of sergeant.

43. See note 6 above.

44. Mannerheim died at Lausanne on January 28, 1951.

45. Tikkanen makes a play on the common and inaccurate political term "to Finlandize," that is, to turn a small neighboring country into a harmless and acquiescent ally without employing great force.

46. Joel Rinne (1897–1981) was one of the leading performers on the Finnish stage. In his later years, he was known for his performance of the role of the elderly Mannerheim in the play *Päämajassa* (*At Headquarters*, 1966), by Ilmaria Turja (1901– ), which was also turned into a film.

47. Gustave III ruled Sweden from 1771 to 1792. An example of the kind of officer referred to here would be G. M. Sprengtporten (1740–1819), who left Swedish service for Russia and served against Sweden's troops in Finland in 1788–89.

48. Tikkanen alludes to the second canto of *Fänrik Stål*, where the poet meets the feigned narrator, a veteran of the war of 1808–1809, and is introduced: "Who'll join me on the road I take/ To Näsijärvi's dusky lake" (Stork's translation, p. 20).

49. Medicine used for the treatment of alcoholism.

50. *Christ and Magdalene*, by Albert Edelfelt (1854–1905), is from 1890; it hangs in the Ateneum at Helsinki. The painting was inspired by the ballad "Mataleena, neito nuori" ("Magdalene, the young maiden"), included in Elias Lönnrot's great collection of folksongs from 1840, the *Kanteletar* (3:5). A translation of a somewhat different version, recorded in Häme in 1879, can be found in Matti Kuusi, Keith Bosley, and Michael Branch, *Finnish Folk Poetry: Epic* (Helsinki: Finnish Literary Society, 1977), pp. 336–38 (Poem 75). The source of the poem is the story of Christ and the Samaritan woman, John 4:7–30.

GEORGE C. SCHOOLFIELD

# Afterword

In the fourth of his books of memoirs, or "autobiographical novels," Henrik Georg Tikkanen (1924–84) paid tribute to the institution with which he had been associated most of his adult life: "I had the press to thank for a great deal, actually for almost everything. I had learned to draw and to write in the service of the newspaper press. The newspapers had given me my public."[1] Characteristically, Tikkanen immediately subjoined a commentary about more doubtful rewards the journalistic world had bestowed: "The newspapers had also been generous with their praise, and when they had been sufficiently generous, they had thought themselves justified in cutting down their praise a little by calling me a drunk, a whoremaster, a boaster about my sexual powers, an exhibitionist, and a bird that dirtied its own nest." Tikkanen had been a well-known public personality in Finland long before his autobiographical suite and his two pacifistic narratives—one of them the present book, *30-åriga kriget* (1977)—gave him both genuine literary stature and an international reputation. From 1947 to 1967, he had worked as a cartoonist and writer of witty aphorisms and columns for the Helsinki Swedish-language morning paper, *Hufvudstadsbladet,* and its now defunct evening-tabloid counterpart, *Nya Pressen;* the nest referred to above is the Swedish-speaking minority in Finland, the so-called Finland-Swedes. After some marked differences of opinion with the management, mordantly described in *Mariegatan 26 Kronohagen* (1977), he changed his home base to the major Finnish-language daily, *Helsingin Sanomat.* Tikkanen had the advantage of being totally bilingual and, from the start of his career, had moved as easily in Finnish journalistic circles as in

Swedish-speaking ones. Besides, his drawings cut straight across language boundaries.

Well into the 1970s, the production of Tikkanen could be described as that of a hyperactive and variously gifted newspaperman. Apart from books where he made the illustrations to someone else's text,[2] there were the travel accounts for which he supplied clever text and skillfully suggestive pictures: *Kär i Stockholm* (*In Love with Stockholm*, 1955),[3] *Paddys land: Irländska skisser* (*Paddy's Land: Irish Sketches*, 1957), *Texas* (1960), *Med bil och barn i Jugoslavien* (*With Car and Kids in Yugoslavia*, 1961), *På jakt efter etruskerna* (*In Search of the Etruscans*, 1967), *I Soviet* (*In the Soviet Union*, 1969), *Dödens Venedig* (*Death's Venice*, 1973), and *Med ett leende i Toscana* (*With a Smile in Tuscany*, 1981). Then there were the collections made of his causeries, where—with his self-ironizing and yet self-laudatory wit and his sharp eye for the manifold sillinesses of everyday life—he showed how close he was to the great Finland-Swedish journalist from the last years of Russian rule in Finland, Gustaf (Guss) Mattsson (1873–1914). Tikkanen issued in book form *Bilbiten: Kåserier på fyra hjul* (*Car-struck:*[4] *Chats on Four Wheels*, 1956), in which he revealed his passion for the automobile as esthetic object and means to (often comical) adventure; *Henrik tiger inte* (*Henrik Won't Be Still*, 1962), using his first name and familiar newspaper signature in the title; *Den stora skandalen* (*The Great Scandal*, 1963), with its splendid and very Mattssonian sketch, "Scorned" (the author—"why wasn't I as good as the next man?"—tells how, on Helsinki's Boulevard, he was the only prosperous-looking pedestrian *not* approached by a beggar); and *Gapa snällt* (*Open Nicely, Please*, 1965), a translation of a Finnish original.[5] A collection of his aphorisms, begun as column-fillers but become something more, appeared in 1970 as *Tankstreck* ("Dashes," literally "Thought-Lines" or "Thought-Marks"): "So much courage is required from a conscientious objector that he ought to make an excellent soldier" and "The most difficult thing in the wars of our present day is to find a good cause to die for."[6] (Tikkanen has told how the production of such unsettling sentences became second nature to him; he could note them down while waiting for a traffic light to change.) Finally, associated with this large oeuvre written originally for diurnal consumption by a broad public, there were the books (with drawings, like the travel books) inspired by two Finnish locales. One was the summertime land of the skerries; *Över fjärden är himlen hög* (*Above the Bay the Sky is High*, 1959) and *Min älskade skärgård* (*My Beloved Skerries*, 1968) have been praised by Gustaf Widén, in his eulogy for the "irreplaceable Tikkanen,"[7] as a part of Tikkanen's heritage from the affectionate satire of Albert Engström (1869–1940), the Swede who—with the same double gift, of drawing and writing, as Tikkanen—became a king of his country's comic newspapers, and a Swedish classic. The other is Tikkanen's home town: in 1972, Tikkanen brought out *Mitt Helsingfors* (*My Helsinki*). The title is borrowed from a verse collection of 1913 by another sometime notable in Finland-Swedish journalistic and belletristic life, Ture Janson (1886–1954), who also (in 1926) published a guidebook to the city; but Tikkanen's volume is largely a set of reflections on his many acquaintances—his drawings take care of the streets and buildings and parks. And it is a preparatory study, in its still somewhat guarded personal allusions, for the "address-novels" begun four years later.

The suite began with *Brändövägen 8 Brändö Tel. 35,*[8] the account Tikkanen gives of his family history and of his own life, from the days of his gestation (he attended the Olympic Games of 1924 in his mother's belly) to the aftermath of the so-called Continuation War with Russia.[9] A book by another rebellious member of the Finland-Swedish patriciate, Christer Kihlman's *Mänskan som skalv* (*The Man Who Trembled*, 1971), had already broken certain taboos about personal revelation (and had shown, as well, how keen public interest was in skeletons released from the closet). Tikkanen might seem to have followed in Kihlman's footsteps as he assailed the snobbish shams, such as they were, of the Finland-Swedish establishment; but his tone, in fact, was altogether different.[10] Kihlman's exposure of himself (and his wife) seemed to be mostly contemporaneous and personally therapeutic, and was recited with a kind of pedagogical earnestness; Tikkanen gladly gave an account of his family's past grandeurs and miseries (and those of its friends) before getting around to his own, and, while doing so, was vastly and intentionally amusing. His paternal great-grandfather had been Paavo Tikkanen (1823–73), the scion of a well-to-do peasant family and a central figure in the establishment of Finland-language literature and, more directly, the Finnish-language press. This forebear, who died insane, had married the granddaughter, "a Swedish upper-class girl," of Johan Jakob Tengström (1755–1832), professor of theology at Åbo Akademy and archbishop. Tikkanen was particularly proud of his relationship to Tengström (when he and his brothers divided his father's estate, he took the portraits of Tengström and his family, the brothers took the apartment), and liked to be photographed with Tengström's sternly handsome face as a backdrop. After the Swedish-Russian War of 1808–1809, in which Russia got Finland, Tengström had advised his fellow countrymen to get along with the victors— advice contrary to that trumpeted later on (in Tikkanen's rough-and-ready interpretation) by the national poet, Johan Ludvig Runeberg, who had married Tengström's niece. "For a long time, [Tengström] was regarded as a traitor. He made peace in a hopeless situation. . . . Bold stupidity created heroes who were worshipped, but wisdom which saved the country could not be forgiven. That is why Runeberg chose to glorify stupidity and became a national poet."[11]

Tengström's great-grandson, and Paavo Tikkanen's son, Johan Jakob Tikkanen (1857–1930) became a favorite of his Runeberg inlaws, and was encouraged in his artistic interests by the poet's eldest son, the sculptor Walter Runeberg (1838–1920); he became the founder of the discipline of art history in Finland, having willingly abandoned his own creative ambitions ("he said that he did not want to increase the number of mediocre artists by adding another" [*Brändövägen 8*, p. 11]). The learned Tikkanen enjoyed an unusually harmonious marriage, to the daughter of a Finland-Swedish lieutenant colonel in the Russian army (and a master marksman); Augusta Emilia Tikkanen, *née* Westzynthius, was a beauty (done in marble by the younger Runeberg), save that she had been born with only one arm: "it is possible that grandfather, who had a Finnish name, would not have got to wed such a fine Swedish girl if she hadn't had this small defect." A productive scholar and a popular lecturer, Professor Tikkanen built a villa in the new and elegant Helsinki island suburb of Brändö (Finnish: Kuulosaari); when he was seventy, he was killed by a car there, "thus becoming Brändö's first traffic fatality." His son, Toivo Robert Tikkanen, Henrik Georg's father, was a would-be singer and an unsuccessful architect and businessman, and a targetshooter who failed to win a medal at Paris in 1924. He married three times: the first wife, the daughter of a wealthy candy manufacturer, died in childbirth, leaving him three sons; his second wife, Henrik Georg's mother, was "not as good as she was beautiful," and the union ended in divorce; a third marriage was soured by Toivo Robert's alcoholism. Tikkanen himself was reared in part by his maternal grandparents, whom he deeply admired and loved, and in part by his father and paternal grandmother. All these people and many others appear in *Brändövägen 8*, portrayed perhaps—as Tikkanen later said, in self-criticism—without an effort to find the deeper cause of their fortunes or misfortunes, but captured with a quick portraiture that makes them quite unforgettable. Unfortunate some of them surely were: Toivo Robert, expelled from his club, died a broken man; Henrik Georg's mother, who once had had "the most beautiful legs in Helsinki," went to wrack and ruin; his eldest half-brother killed himself while on leave during Finland's Winter War; the other half-brothers, twins, likewise died early, one of heart disease (after a hectic career as a salesman), the other, an artist, as a suicide.

In the suite's next volumes (*Bävervägen 11 Hertonäs* [1976] and *Mariegatan 26 Kronohagen* [1977]), Tikkanen tells about his own growing dependence on drink ("In such moments I felt like Hemingway"), his continental journeys with the left-wing poet Arvo Turtiainen, his efforts to establish himself as a newspaper cartoonist, his unimpassioned first marriage (solemnized under the aegis of a presidential couple from the 1920s, Kaarlo and Esther Ståhlberg), and his long affair with the woman who then became his second wife, and who may be responsible for having awakened his serious literary ambitions: "She loved words and she never forgot what she had seen written; I talked and talked, but it was like an English fire, the heat went up the chimney. . . . I was astounded by the power of words."[12] Like their predecessor, these books have as their titles key addresses in their author's life; Brändö is followed by the monotonous bedroom suburb of Hertonäs/Herttoniemi ("we worked at marriage the way you do at a business"), to be replaced by Kronohagen/Kruununhaka, the old section of the capital where he settled down with Märta Tikkanen, née Cavonius. In *Georgsgatan* (1980), then, Tikkanen uses a street where the gallery is located in which an exhibition of his art is to be held. The street holds memories: his old gymnasium had stood there (its site now adorned by a fountain, with a sculpture of a woman astride a dragon: "She had my mother's legs—my mother had been married to the sculptor" [*Georgsgatan*, p. 37]); the movie house to which his father had taken him as a child ("how proud I was") survives, together with the little theater that produced his play "Fjäriln" ("The Butterfly") about his father's weaknesses. The main material of *Georgsgatan*, however, is contemporary, about his "daughter's" almost mortal illness and her miraculous recovery (the "daughter" was, in fact, one of Tikkanen's sons), about the diagnosis of the illness that would kill him five years later, and about the beloved wife who has become a spokeswoman for woman's rights. (In her own best-seller, *Århundradets kärlekssaga* [*The Love Story of the Cen-*

*tury,* 1978],[13] Märta Tikkanen described his numerous failings, notably his dipsomania and his egotism.)

The final book in the street-address series, *Henriksgatan* (1982), bears Tikkanen's first name, as *Georgsgatan* did his middle one. Henriksgatan is the old name of Mannerheimvägen/Mannerheimintie, the main thoroughfare on which lie the editorial offices of *Hufvudstadsbladet* and *Helsingin Sanomat*—as well as Stockman's, the great department store where he was taken to buy Dinky Toys as a child. The book's form is quasi-diaristic, reflections set down on each of the fifty days of the abstention from journalism the author has to enter during his service as elector *in spe* during the Finnish presidential campaign of 1982. In it, again, his thoughts circle around the wife whose literary star has been rapidly rising ("I have given her a fruitful hell in which she, like Dante, becomes all-embracing")[14] and his Tikkanen grandparents (he has come across correspondence from their Roman sojourn of the 1880s) and the political world in which he is both participant and observer. Finally, if *Henriksgatan* has the air of a diary (or a very personal daily newspaper column), Tikkanen's *Renault, mon amour: En autobiografi* (1983),[15] is a more traditional book of memories—the cars in his life, and the pleasures of automobile travel in Europe of the 1950s, when highways were uncrowded and Tikkanen was young. As always, his thoughts go to his progenitors—his grandfathers (the one run down by a woman driver, the other crushed in his official limousine at a grade crossing) and his father, who met his mother one day in the early 1920s. "The maiden, pretty as a picture, lived in a small town and was in love with a young man, likewise pretty as a picture, when father appeared. He came driving up in a Reo Flying Cloud which, like the heavenly trumps, proclaimed his potency, and in his mouth he had a thick Havana cigar which imparted the remaining information. Mama grew giddy and fell under his spell, for nothing of the sort had ever been seen in the little town before" (p. 11). *Renault, mon amour* returned, incidentally, to Tikkanen's practice of combining text with illustration; on pages 11–12 one sees a double-page drawing of the Flying Cloud, flanked by his lovely mother ("You could think the fashions of the 1920s were made expressly for her") and his father, the *soi-disant* "Devil's friend," foot on running board and cheroot in hand.

Tikkanen shied away from calling his personal accounts autobiographies;[16] in *Henriksgatan*, the journal-keeper reproves his daughter, who has just informed him that he ought to stop writing about himself. "I have written twenty-five books dealing with myself in world history, but the five which deal with me in the present are fiction" (p. 97). The answer is both jesting and evasive (what indeed are the five books dealing with Tikkanen in the present: the address-novels?). Surely most of his work has been remarkably self-centered, with the exception of his first attempt at a comic fable and the two books about the forgotten sentinel, Viktor Käppärä, *30-åriga kriget* and *Efter hjältedöden*. The debut book, *Mr. Gogo kommer till Europa* (*Mr. Gogo Comes to Europe,* 1946), was described by Tikkanen in *Bävervägen 11* (p. 46) as "an innocent and childish story[17] about an ape which, arriving in Europe as an African cultural attaché, discovers that capitalism leads to war and oppression and that fascism is insanity, pure and simple." Tikkanen then waited for fifteen years to try his hand at the novel again; *Hjältarna är döda* (*The Heroes Are Dead,* 1961)[18] describes the *vie de Bohème* of Tom, a would-be artist in Helsinki the first year after the armistice with Russia. With the hindsight provided by the address-novels, one can readily make out that Tom is Henrik Georg, that the drunken and humiliated father ("Immoderation was my ruin") is Toivo Robert and the faithless mother the once lovely Kylliki Tikkanen: she has had an affair with a powerful politician ("He's a man of honor. If he had been your father, you'd never have had to go to the front"). Today, *Hjältarna är döda* is best read together with *Bävervägen 11*, and in the knowledge that *Mitt Helsingfors* of 1972 forms a kind of intermediate confessional stage between the two. For example, the episode about the "homosexual theater director's" method of dealing with a nosy policeman in the novel (pp. 154–55) is retold in the Helsinki "guidebook," but with the editor Antti Halonen as its main figure; while another figure in the same episode, the student who hates Communists and homosexuals (and is then seduced by the theater director) turns up again in *Bävervägen 11*, accompanied by a fuller account of his fate (pp. 44–45). Likewise, the Casanovan tale of Tom's sexual record-setting with "Gigi" (*Hjältarna*, pp. 121–29) returns in *Bävervägen 11*, the *mise-en-scène* somewhat changed; Tom's love affair with the "respectable girl, Gittan," reappears as the story of Brita, begun in *Brändövägen 8* and brought to its sadly gruesome end in *Bävervägen 11*.

Just so, in the next novel *Ödlorna* (*The Lizards*, 1965),[19] a sequel of sorts to *Hjältarna är döda*, the symbolic episode of the burning of the lizards, used epanaleptically in the novel, introduces the theme of senseless cruelty in *Brändövägen 8* (p. 27); war memories tormenting the novel's narrator come back in one or another of the autobiographical volumes—for example, the sight of the soldier, the back of whose head has been blown away (*Ödlorna*, p. 12, *Brändövägen 8*, p. 104), or the indecent advances of the German commissary officer (*Ödlorna*, pp. 21–25, *Bävervägen 11*, p. 43), or the sadism of the company commander (*Ödlorna*, pp. 61–65, *Brändövägen 8*, pp. 103, 107–16). The narrator's father is a boastful drunk whose one military deed was to shoot from his balcony at fleeing members of the Red Guard during the Civil War (*Ödlorna*, p. 15, *Brändövägen 8*, p. 20), and his mother is promiscuous ("My mother betrayed my father solely with cavalry officers" [*Ödlorna*, p. 15]); the narrator's postwar Mediterranean adventures are undertaken in the company of the poet Arno (see Arvo Turtiainen in *Bävervägen 11*), and Maria, the Genoese prostitute who falls in love with the young man in *Ödlorna*, returns in *Bävervägen 11*, still working at the Trocadero Bar.

As a matter of fact, even Tikkanen's last novel, *TTT* (1979),[20] cannot let go of the immediate postwar years; it comprises the memories—inspired by present marital problems—of the middle-aged artist "Tott," Tor Torsten Torsson, "sexist pig, drunk, whoremaster, and exhibitionist," about his experiences—not least sexual ones—as a Finnish war veteran in Stockholm of the 1940s. Like the narrator of *Ödlorna* and the Tikkanen of *Bävervägen 11*, young Tott also goes to Italy, making his headquarters this time, however, in Venice. (Another Venetian visit, fifteen years later, is superimposed upon Tott's recollections of the first one; the latter journey bears a strong resemblance—"only after he had visited Harry's Bar where Hemingway drank did he really begin to drink as Hemingway had drunk" [p. 120]—to the nightmarish and heavily alcoholized Venetian stay with which *Mariegatan 26* ends.) Not even so devoted an admirer of Tikkanen's work as Gustaf Widén can find much good to say about the novel ("Tikkanen could well have refrained from tossing off such a book as *TTT*"), and Thomas Warburton wrote, not unfairly, that Tikkanen had "lost his way in a labyrinth of ego from which the books about Viktor Käppärä have offered the only exit, until now."[21] Of course, Warburton could not know that Tikkanen's career was almost over; now, after his death, one can guess that TTT's nickname is a pun of sorts on the German "Tod" or "tot." (However, it also suggests the name of a great Swedish noble family.) The last book to appear under Tikkanen's flag, *De nakna och de saliga*[22] (*The Naked and the Blest*, 1983), had texts by Christer Kihlman and drawings by Tikkanen—drawings, in this emblem-book of erotica, where the male lover is often given death's features, leading the mind to Holbein's *Der Tod und das Mädchen*.

It could be proposed that, in the three narratives from 1946 to 1965, *Mr. Gogo* and *Hjältarna är döda* and *Ödlorna*, Tikkanen worked his way backward, toward his own army experiences: the little satire talks about naïve hopes, of which Gogo is disabused, the Bohemian novel about a return to civilian life (one learns nothing about Tom's military service), the lizard-novel about a melange of battlefield and travel memories. It was not until *Brändövägen 8* of 1976 that Tikkanen confronted the war head-on. But two years earlier he had published a novel in Finnish, *Unohdettu sotilas (Forgotten Soldier)*,[23] in which he described the fate of another young soldier who survived. (Is there any significance in the fact that Tikkanen, still attempting to hold the war at a distance, wrote his novel in a language which, although he commanded it perfectly, was not his mother tongue, or, as Kierkegaard would have said, "the language of his heart"? "It was not only alcohol I bore so poorly, and more poorly the older I got; war made me sick too" [*Mariegatan 26*, p. 101]). Whatever the circumstances surrounding the genesis of *Unohdettu sotilas* may have been, the immediate spark for the tale is easily detected. In March, 1974, a Japanese lieutenant, Hiroo Onoda, fifty-two years old, was persuaded to leave the Philippine jungles where he had held out for the past twenty-nine years; his presence had been known to the authorities since 1954, several searches had been conducted for him, and he had twice been declared dead. His "surrender" had been preceded, in January, 1972, by that of Sergeant Shoichi Yokoi on Guam. Both Lieutenant Onoda and Sergeant Yokoi were aware that the war had long since ended; the lieutenant thought himself bound by a Japanese military code that preferred death to surrender.[24]

*Unohdettu sotilas* is not a particularly successful work of art, in good part because it spends too little time with Vihtori (Viktor) Käppärä—left behind at an outpost in the North Karelian wilderness on the last day of the war, staying at his post in obedience to the order of his admired sergeant, Johannes Hurmalainen—and too much with an involved subplot concerning other characters in the world outside (characters then reduced in importance or deleted in the second, Swedish version of 1977). The anonymous "long-haired Stalinist (naturally from the land's most conservative right-wing paper)" has both a name and a clearly defined job in version one: he is Mikko Lahtinen, an editor of the (liberal) *Helsingin Sanomat*, involved in an adulterous liaison with Anneli Haukinen, the neglected wife of the ambitious Colonel J. P. Haukinen, an officer determined to bring Käppärä back alive. Haukinen discovers that Anneli has promised to pass along details of the action to the newspaperman (who, in his turn, sends Haukinen a copy of a "Mata-Hari letter" from Anneli, thereby threatening informational blackmail). Feeling that his soldier's honor has been besmirched and his career ruined, Haukinen hangs himself—after Lahtinen has been shot by Käppärä for having pilfered the brassiere Viktor regards as "his woman." There are other signs of an all too heavy hand, such as the message (in English) which one "Richard" sends Viktor in the basket of provisions the obstinate sentry retrieves from the helicopter he has downed: "Never give up." (One may well think of Richard Nixon's stubborn clinging to a lie, and to the White House, in Watergate days.) At novel's end, Viktor dies of a heart attack during the attack by Captain Matalamäki's forces (with their blank bullets) on his little stronghold; and his corpse is saluted by the pompous general-of-infantry, Kaarle S. Ruohonen, who (at the order of Defense Minister Göös) has taken over the conduct of the steadily more painful Käppärä affair.[25] Lyydia Käppärä, Viktor's mother—much more is told about the Käppärä parents in the Finnish version—is informed of the death of her son, in whose survival she had not wanted to believe at any rate, having long ago made up her mind that he had fallen in the war: "Viktor's mother said she had not doubted it for a minute."

Another shortcoming of *Unohdettu sotilas* may lie in Tikkanen's difficulties with his main character; he does not know quite what to do with him in his isolation. A solution to which he comes (dropped in the Swedish version) is to give him a certain modest intellectual ballast; as a boy in the skerries, Viktor had read *Robinson Crusoe*, and in his imagination he devises a Friday-figure, a by no means satisfactory friend, who shares his hermitage with him for a while. In the Swedish version, Käppärä becomes still more the almost unlettered and inexperienced innocent, thinking—when not engaged in the sexual fantasies for which Lisa and Hurmalainen's tales have provided the meager stuff—of his mother. One of the more pathetic (and, in the Swedish version, narratively very useful) details concerning the way he passes time in the wilderness is that of his letter-writing; the government investigators, the official biographers, and the reader get most of their knowledge about Viktor from those unposted epistles to "Mama." (Tikkanen himself recalled that, at the front, it was not a sense of comradeship that kept him going. "It was my mother's letters. She wrote a letter every day, hundreds of letters" [*Georgsgatan*, pp. 111–12];[26] and one has to conclude that Private Tikkanen replied.)

It is only in the story of the maternal correspondence—and in a sense of isolation—that Käppärä seems to have much in common with Tikkanen; Käppärä may seem an example of the loyal and not very bright soldier, while Tikkanen's manifold problems in the military came from the circumstance that he thought too much (unlike his older twin brothers, he says, who were slow learners in school and excellent men-at-arms). "I was not as credulous as the peasant boys in my company. They were all at least a couple of years older than I, but they believed that war was like frost, it came when it came. . . . If the military operation failed and half of them fell, then it was the frost which had taken its share; God and the commander bore no blame for what happened, since both of them, after all, were on our side. They were incomparable soldiers, as the Marshal expressed it" (*Brändövägen 8*, p. 112). Elsewhere, Tikkanen enlarged upon his loneliness as a young soldier: "I had never had a real friend. . . . the war came and I was always the youngest, and the soldier who is youngest and a volunteer besides is always regarded with suspicion.[27] Matters were not improved by the fact that I was the only private in my company who had taken the student's examination [and so was qualified to attend university]. At the front, education meant estrangement from the enlisted men, and the educated officers in their turn did not associate with ordinary soldiers. I had a lonely war" (*Bävervägen 11*, pp. 80–81).

What had happened to Tikkanen was this: in his early teens,

his mother (influenced by her passion for cavalry officers) had him take riding lessons, and he became "in truth a very good equestrian," getting a trophy from the hand of General Hugo Österman himself, the commander of Finland's armed forces. "The step from the riding school to the civilian defense corps was not a large one" (*Brändövägen 8*, p. 68), and "at the age of fourteen I got a weapon in my hand . . . the same weapon as that used in the Russian-Japanese War, and it strengthened my impression of the permanence of the ideals I was to fight for" (*Georgsgatan*, p. 39). Late in the autumn of 1939, he fired (quite in vain) at the Russian bombers attacking Helsinki, in the opening act of the Winter War. After the Continuation War had begun, in June, 1941, he joined a boys' company of the Patriotic Front, led by his teacher, Guido Simberg, and "went to look for Russian agents behind the lines" in the newly recaptured parts of Finnish Karelia. In this paramilitary capacity he got to see Lake Ladoga, but, as he stooped to drink of "its holy waters," he saw the swollen corpse of a Russian soldier floating close by and "realized that war also had its unesthetic sides." Back at school, he embroidered his experiences of "battle," and eventually, taking his finals in 1943, managed to enter the tradition-rich regiment "Nyland's Dragoons, Mannerheim's old unit," as a volunteer. "I dreamt of riding into Petersburg and Moscow while the liberated populace cheered" (*Brändövägen 8*, p. 102). Unhappily, Tikkanen adds, the regiment soon abandoned its horses for bicycles. Bored with life behind the lines, Tikkanen got himself switched to the front; there he became the special prey of a vicious company commander, from whose clutches he eventually escaped by a transfer to the brigade staff as a cartographer. He was present at the Russian breakthrough on the Karelian Isthmus in June, 1944 ("I saw the wave of panic the military police, who shot down fleeing soldiers, could not stop" [*Brändövägen 8*, p. 118]); somewhere near Summa, southeast of Viipuri, "I settled my accounts with the war, which had first seemed to be an exciting adventure, but then proved itself to be a lamentable mistake" (*Brändövägen 8*, p. 118). He wounded himself in the arm, "a shameful deed which made me into a man. I had taken my fate into my own hands" (p. 121). Yet, recovering quickly, he was sent back to the front; "on the last day of the war, I got dysentery." Calling him a coward, the officer in charge of his position refused him permission to go to a field hospital, but "blood, my blood, gave me courage and confidence just the same, and I set out toward the medical corpsman. It was a couple of kilometers to the hospital hut, and it took me hours, for I was able to drag myself along only a few dozen yards at a time. . . . The next morning when I awoke in my blood-soaked cot, there was peace between Finland and the Soviet Union. I had escaped from the war alive, but the war had soured the rest of my life. We were quits" (*Mariegatan 26*, pp. 80–81). The armistice that ended the fighting took place on September 4, 1944; Tikkanen had his twentieth birthday five days later.

Now, the differences between Private Tikkanen and Private Käppärä are quite plain. Apart from his foolish desire to be a soldier (sprung up, he says, "in the militarily infected atmosphere" of the later 1930s), Tikkanen was something of a sophisticate (and sexually experienced), the child of a distinguished family that had friends in high places (although they could not get him what he wanted, a post as a sketcher at the front), and, in short order, a skeptic whose "individualism," as he later called it, got him charged by his company commander with defeatism. Käppärä, on the other hand, has come from a simple and lonely life on the skerries, has evidently waited to be drafted, and, after three months of training in Ostrobothnia, has been sent off to what seems to be a relatively quiet section of the line, there to be taken under the kindly wing of Sergeant Hurmalainen. Tikkanen had long been aware that the war was lost; Käppärä apparently does not realize—on the last day of the war—that the Soviet army is about to triumph. During his long years of isolation, he believes instead that the war will end in the final victory Mannerheim had promised: "when Karelia was liberated, the

Field Marshal would sheath his sword just as he'd pledged to do. Viktor decided that he'd fire off a rocket. What troubled him a little was that he'd never remembered to ask the sergeant which side of the border they were on. But it didn't really matter—as long as the new border of Greater Finland would be far to the east, along the Urals or at least from Ladoga to the White Sea." Reading about the Korean War in the newspaper fragments in the cottage he has burned (and whose inhabitants he has killed), Viktor concludes that Finnish troops are about to throw the Communists into the Pacific as an end to the long conflict. In short, Viktor is remarkably stupid, or, in a kindlier phrase, naïve.

It will be remembered that Tikkanen praised his ancestor, Archbishop Tengström, and denigrated his distant in-law, Runeberg, because the latter chose to glorify stupidity "and became the national poet." The passage in *Bävervägen 11* goes on to say that the nation once again, following "the spirit of Sven Dufva," had beaten its brow bloody against the Russians; only after 1944 had it realized that the clever, practical-minded, and conciliatory Tengström was right. In some ways, it would be simple enough to interpret Käppärä as a reincarnation of Runeberg's dull-witted hero from *Fänrik Stål* who held a bridge against all odds: "A sorry head Sven Dufva had; his heart, though, that was good." In his distrust of what he takes as Finland's foes and in his bloody defense of his fortifications in the woods, Käppärä behaves as a Sven Dufva would. The official biographers of Käppärä are not, in fact, to be seriously criticized for their giving a Runebergian cast to their description of the brave sentinel; Käppärä might appear to have lived up perfectly to Runeberg's description of the Finnish soldier in still another of his epyllia, *Julkvällen* (*Christmas Eve*, 1841): "Artless, earnest, and calm, with an iron-hard honor within him," a representative of the Finnish people, whose "faithfulness defies death," as Ensign Stål tells his young admirer in what is perhaps the most famous of Runeberg's set pieces about the war of 1808–1809 against the Russians, "The Fifth of July." Like Väinö Linna with his numerous allusions to Runeberg in his novel of the Continuation War, *Tuntematon sotilas* (*Unknown Soldier*, 1955), Tikkanen remembers that his immediate audience knows its Runeberg. In Linna, the soldiers themselves quote Runeberg, often quite mangled, on inappropriately appropriate occasions (for example, seeing the mutilated corpse of a Russian who has killed himself with a hand grenade, a Finnish soldier thinks of the opening of "Number 15 Stolt": "The handsome day had reached its end," and of "Döbeln at Jutas": "Döbeln rode before thinning ranks"); in Tikkanen, the narrator's voice, expressly or by suggestion, calls Runeberg again and again to the reader's mind.

A major discrepancy exits, nonetheless, between a Dufva (or a "Number 15 Stolt") and Käppärä, a discrepancy made apparent at the novel's very outset, and a discrepancy that, in its turn, reveals Käppärä as a brother under the skin to Private Tikkanen. To Runeberg (who had never heard a shot fired in anger or done a day of military service), it was fair and fitting, *dulce et decorum*, to die for one's country; the girl who has lost her heroic lover on the battlefield in "The Cloud's Brother" sums it up: "Sweeter far than life I found that love was,/ Sweeter far than love to die as he did." But Käppärä has learned an opposed lesson from Hurmalainen[28]—a soldier's first duty is to stay alive. That is why Käppärä stayed at his post; "the most intelligent soldiers stay where they are, hoping not to be forced to advance *or* retreat, and also that the heaviest combat areas will occur somewhere far, far away. If one is lucky that can actually happen. It was in this hope that Viktor stayed at his post and became a national hero." And Käppärä also has the order from Hurmalainen to which he can refer, he thinks, if questioned about his behavior. It is to these thoughts that Viktor returns in his letters later on: "He did not want to run after the advancing army and expose himself to the manifold dangers of the attack, and he could not go home either. Then he would be taken and shot as a deserter. All that was left was to stay at his post and wait to be relieved." It may at first seem a weakness in Tikkanen's characterization that Käppärä, unthinking in so much, has reasoned out this manner of survival so carefully; yet this glimmering of intelligence on Käppärä's part points up the book's irony. The innocent Käppärä, grasping an essential lesson of survival, is turned into a murderer by the lesson, a transformation abetted, again, by the rules of military life he has learned and the propaganda he has absorbed—all this as a participant in a war long since over. (And the man who has saved his life these last thirty years has in fact lost or wasted it.)

Yet there is no getting away from the Runebergian (or Sven Dufva–like) quality in Käppärä, as it is revealed in his stubbornness and his inability to extend his thoughts beyond certain limits; he has a predecessor in the comic novel of Finland, in the soldier Joose Keppilä of Veijo Meri's *Manillaköysi* (*The Manila Rope*, 1957), who almost dies from his efforts to bring home something of value—a manila rope—from the front. The rope has been wrapped too tightly around Joose's body, and the soldiers' tales told on the leave train (where Joose, the hero of the frame-story, sits slowly expiring) likewise have to do with the often mortal and certainly silly results of obstinacy and lack of imagination. Joose's rope, cut from his swollen body at the book's end, is itself ruined.

Viktor's pigheadedness is turned to better ends in the sequel, *Efter hjältdöden* (*After the Hero's Death*) of 1977.[29] Surviving the attack on his dugout, he enters the contemporary world, a kind of Rip Van Winkle. Inadvertently he becomes a television star, but his impresario, Calle Sjöman, has difficulties in making the real Viktor jibe with the prettified Runebergian image (in the style of Runeberg's "The Cloud's Brother" or "Vilhelm von Schwerin") that the nation has constructed: "The Finns were put off by reality. All too often it had turned out to be unpleasant. And the living Viktor also looked wretched; Calle had to admit that. False teeth would help out a little, of course. But his shifty glance and his fidgety movements, what could be done about them? A hero was the way Runeberg had described him, calm and nice-looking even with his breast perforated by bullets. A horrible falsification of reality which [Finland's] three wars had not succeeded in changing. Just as the image of Runeberg himself was falsified, nobody wanted to hear about the poet who was a domestic tyrant, a whoremaster, a drunk, a tormenter of his wife, a warmonger" (*Efter hjältedöden*, p. 65). So great is the contrast between reality and ideal that the public refuses to believe Viktor is indeed the forgotten hero of Tuokojärvi, and he must be presented as a comical figure, "a parody of a hero." The sometime girl of his onanistic dreams, Lisa, attends one of his performances and denies categorically that the clownish figure is "her beloved Viktor"; threatened by a mob, Viktor is spirited away, yet manages to escape from his savior (Calle's henchman), and—by remarkable coincidence—finds his way to the home of Johannes Hurmalainen.

His whereabouts betrayed to Calle by Jenny, Hurmalainen's feminist termagant of a wife, Viktor still cannot prove that he is what he says he is; but Hurmalainen, quicker witted, reminds him of his dogtag, which he still wears. Now he can be accepted by the public as himself, but a new difficulty arises. At a public interview with his official biographers (commissioned, of course, to portray him as a Runebergian figure), Viktor proves that they have omitted the section of a letter to his mother in which he made no bones about his self-preservatory intent in remaining at his post; he quotes the letter from memory: "Hurmalainen has said that this is the safest place in the whole damned war. No enemy will come this way. . . . I'd be crazy if I ran away from here and got myself killed to no good purpose. The order Hurmalainen gave me is my life insurance" (pp. 119–20). Viktor and Hurmalainen are taken into protective custody and submitted to psychiatric investigation; in order to carry out a plan he has conceived while taking refuge with Hurmalainen (the illumination came to him as he worked on a church tower), Viktor agrees with his psychiatrists that "his antipathy to being a hero did not change the fact that he was a hero" (p. 125). Offers from all over the world rain down upon him—to appear in the advertisements of munitions and aircraft syndicates, to let Hollywood make a film about him, to permit *Playboy* to write his memoirs in return for a million dollars. He is invited to stand on Lenin's tomb on May 1, to appear as the guest of honor at 87 Rotary Clubs in the United States, to speak at 320 patriotic societies at home and abroad. "Finland's national bank wanted to make him chairman of the board, and Idi Amin named him an honorary citizen of Uganda" (p. 130).

Calle Sjöman decides to begin the latest phase of Viktor's career by letting him appear at a youth festival in Helsinki; in a *coup de théâtre* (and in a speech both extremely long and well-turned to have come from the verbally ungifted Viktor), the hero reveals his scheme for universal demilitarization. The idea's popularity spreads so rapidly that "responsible statesmen and military men" grow anxious; a "thoroughly democratized world" is unacceptable. At a meeting of the Socialist International in Madrid, Viktor is assassinated as he shakes hands with Sweden's Olof Palme. "After a week had passed, the CIA reported that, through its contacts with the underworld, it had succeeded in ferreting out the information that the hired assassin had actually aimed at Palme, but missed" (p. 136).[30] From this résumé, it will be seen that the latter part of the sequel to *30-åriga kriget* has turned into sermonizing, and Viktor into a kind of Christ. When Viktor, rediscovered, set out on the final tour with Calle, leading to his peace mission and his death, Jenny Hurmalainen counted the reward Sjöman had given her: "The woman who had sold the savior of the world for 5,000 marks sat in her kitchen, drinking coffee with doughnuts, and without the slightest trace of a bad conscience" (p. 113).

Tikkanen's ironic message is unexceptionable, but the instructive joke—begun with the forgetting of Viktor Käppärä on the final day of the Continuation War—has lost its salt. One could say that, in *30-åriga kriget*, Tikkanen wrote the last of those several comical tales, making bitter points, that grew out of the

northern sideshow of World War II. The tradition was begun
with Pentti Haanpää's (1905–55) set of stories about the fate of a
pair of soldier's boots, *Yhdeksän miehen saappaat (The Boots of
Nine Men*, 1945), and continued by Veijo Meri in any number of
his works and—in Swedish—by Tikkanen's friend, the artist
Rolf Sandqvist (1919– ), in *Mitt kära krig (My Dear War*, 1967).
The dear war afforded quite sufficient cause for baffled laughter,
if the awful suffering it entailed could be forgotten. After all, it
was a conflict in which the Marshal of Finland could shake hands
with Adolf Hitler, as his fellow protector of Western cultural
values; a conflict during which the United States did not declare
war against Finland although Finland had invaded the Soviet
Union, America's ally of the time; a conflict that had Finnish
soldiers of Jewish extraction serving beside German troops, as
the novelist Daniel Katz has remarked. It was a conflict that got
odd reactions in odd places; Guy Crouchback, Evelyn Waugh's
mouthpiece in *The End of the Battle*, tells his father (and they are
both honorable and good men) that England lost its moral bearings when it declared war on Finland, Russia's enemy: "it
doesn't seem to matter now who wins." Tikkanen's message is
that all war is bad and unnatural; the Continuation War, only the
first stage of poor Viktor Käppärä's Thirty Years' War, was unnatural in the extreme. But unnaturalness can be a good growing
ground for literature.

NOTES

1. *Georgsgatan* (Helsinki: Söderström & Co., 1980), pp. 43–44.

2. *Bilderbok för stora barn (Picture Book for Big Children*, 1951),
*Vi ser på Helsingfors (We Look at Helsinki*, 1952), *Romerska bilder
(Roman Pictures*, 1953), all with his friend Benedikt Zilliacus;
*Isbrytarresa längs Finlands kust (Icebreaker Trip along Finland's
Coast*, 1962), *Utöar (Outer Islands*, 1974).

3. The title offers an example of Tikkanen's ability to pun: it
may also mean "In Love in Stockholm."

4. *Bilbiten* means either "car-bitten" or "the car-bit," that is, a newspaper column about cars.

5. *Kita kiinni*[!] (1965); a number of Tikkanen's other works, including the whole of the autobiographical suite, have appeared in Finnish.

6. *Tankstreck* (Helsinki: Söderström & Co., 1970), pp. 18–19. Later on, for the Stockholm daily *Dagens Nyheter* and the Oslo paper *Dagbladet*, he did a series of sketches of heads, with accompanying texts; some of these were published as *Ansikten och åsikter* (*Faces and Opinions*, 1980).

7. "Den oersättlige Tikkanen," *Finsk Tidskrift* 209–10 (1985): 91–94.

8. (Helsinki: Söderström & Co., 1976); an English translation by Mary Sandbach has appeared as *Snob's Island* (London: Chatto and Windus, 1980) and *A Winter's Day* (New York: Pantheon, 1980).

9. Finland's recent wars bear the following names: Talvisota (Winter War; Swedish: Vinterkrig), with the Soviet Union, from November, 1939, to March, 1940; Jatkosota (Continuation War, Fortsättningskrig), the quasi-continuation of the war with the Soviet Union, from June, 1941, until September, 1944; and Lapin sota (Lapland War, Lapplandskrig), with German troops in northern Finland, from September, 1944, until April, 1945.

10. For a discussion of the phenomenon of Finland-Swedish memoiristic literature, see George C. Schoolfield, " 'The August Light of Abiding Memories': Finland-Swedish Memoir Literature," *World Literature Today* 54 (1980): 15–20.

11. *Bävervägen 11 Hertonäs* (Helsinki: Söderström & Co., 1976), p. 8.

12. *Mariegatan 26 Kronohagen* (Helsinki: Söderström & Co., 1977), pp. 8–9.

13. The book has appeared in English, translated by Stina Katchadourian and published by the Capra Press, Santa Barbara, CA, 1984.

14. *Henriksgatan* (Helsinki: Söderström & Co., 1982), p. 32.

15. (Helsinki: Söderström & Co.). The pun in the title is obvious; the normal Swedish word for "autobiography" is *självbiografi*.

16. Markku Envall, "Henrik Tikkanen: Master of Satire," *Books from Finland* 15 (1981), 1:5–8, gets around the question of genre by speaking of "more or less autobiographical novels or memoirs."

17. In fact, *Mr. Gogo* was followed by two little books for children.

18. (Helsinki: Söderström & Co.).

19. (Helsinki: Söderström & Co.).

20. (Helsinki: Söderström & Co.).

21. Widén, "Den oersättlige Tikkanen"; Thomas Warburton, *Åttio år finlandssvensk litteratur* (Helsinki: Schildt, 1984), p. 406.

22. (Helsinki: Söderström & Co.).

23. (Helsinki: Tammi). Like the Swedish version, *Unohdettu sotilas* contains illustrations by the author; the two sets are not identical.

24. According to the *New York Times* of January 25, 1972. Yokoi said he had "learned about 20 years ago that the war was over but he was afraid to come out of hiding."

25. The illustration (p. 131) shows General Ruohonen saluting Käppärä's body; in *30-åriga kriget* (p. 120 of this translation) a general, drawn in more detail, salutes a hole.

26. In *Brändövägen 8* (p. 120), Tikkanen had said: "I thought of mother. She wrote a letter every day. She cared about me."

27. Tikkanen had already brought the matter up in *Ödlorna* (p. 61): "The platoon I landed in was not enthusiastic about my arrival either. One of the soldiers asked me immediately if I were crazy."

28. Is "Hurmalainen" a talking name? *Hurma* can mean "personal charm" or "attraction," and the verb *hurmata* "to enchant."

29. (Helsinki: Söderström & Co.). A Finnish translation of both Swedish texts, called *Viimeinen sankari* (*The Last Hero*), by Elvi Sinervo, came out in 1979.

30. In the novel by Maj Sjöwall and Per Wahlöö, *Terroristerna* (Stockholm: Norstedt, 1975), the Swedish prime minister is shot by a former "flower child," not by one of the narrative's professional terrorists.